Full Rigged

Rebecca Connolly
Sophia Summers
Heather B. Moore

Full Rigged

LOST ★ CREEK ★ RODEO

Copyright © 2021 by Rebecca Connolly
Print edition
All rights reserved

No part of this book may be reproduced in any form whatsoever without prior written permission of the publisher, except in the case of brief passages embodied in critical reviews and articles. This is a work of fiction. The characters, names, incidents, places, and dialog are products of the author's imagination and are not to be construed as real.

Interior design by Cora Johnson
Edited by Joanne Lui, Lorie Humpherys, and Laramee Fox
Cover design by Rachael Anderson
Cover image credit: Period Images
Published by Mirror Press, LLC

ISBN: 978-1-952611-17-9

Lost Creek Rodeo Series

Round Up
Chute Boss
Rough Stock
Full Rigged
Half Hitch
Ace High

CHAPTER 1

DARREN WAS GOING TO turn this place into the greatest ranch in Montana, no question there. It would take less than three years to implement the changes he had planned, upgrade the equipment, and expand the lands to include some acres up for sale on neighboring properties. And once all of that was done, the sky would be the limit, and not much else.

Ford Hopkins shook his head as he looked at his brother's plans, including the future map of the lands. "Darren, this is good stuff. Real good. If only Dad would let you do it now."

His older brother groaned and folded his arms on the worn desk of his makeshift office. "I know. He keeps telling me he'll hang up his ropes and turn it over, but he's no closer to retiring than John Parks in Fallon."

"He's forty if he's a day," Ford pointed out.

"Exactly." The brothers shared wan smiles.

Ford exhaled heavily, pushing the plans back to his brother. "I'm sorry, man. You've gotta be chompin' at the bit."

"I am," his brother grunted, pushing the sleeves of his

Henley up past his elbows. "Not that I want Dad gone, but he won't let me do anything except work on the ranch, like I've always done."

"Like we've all done." Ford tapped a finger against the desk absently, his mind taking him back to the hours upon hours they had all spent working on the family ranch, raising the cattle, seeing them sorted and sold, branding, calving, driving the truck of hay before they could fully see over the steering wheel . . . They'd done it all from the day they were old enough to obey instructions.

Not all of the siblings had loved it as much as Ford and Darren had, but at least it had raised them up right.

Darren was the oldest son, and since he wanted to take over the ranch, their father was going to sign it over.

Eventually.

Ford wanted the ranch, too—badly—but he wasn't about to get between his brother and his birthright, so to speak.

It had always gone to oldest sons, and Darren's five-year-old boy was already talking about the day the ranch would be his, taking his own chores very seriously on "his ranch," and even volunteering to help mend one of the fences with the men yesterday.

Their younger brother, Tucker, wanted to stay on the ranch as well, but in a much smaller capacity, which Darren would be more than happy to give him. Tuck was great with the cattle and would make his brother an excellent overseer when the time came.

Ford didn't want to answer to anyone on a ranch. Not his father, not his brother, not some outsider taking things over. He wanted to call the shots, make the changes, shoulder the blame, and work by the sweat of his own brow and the calluses on his own hands. He'd clash with Darren daily if he tried to work under him, and he'd never enjoyed confrontation.

In his family, at any rate.

It was one of the reasons he'd been a decent hockey player. His frustrations could be vented on the ice, especially in delivering hard hits, and he had done so. But he'd never really had a future in the sport, not when his heart was in being a cowboy.

So he'd turned to rodeo.

It was an easy enough shift, given he'd competed occasionally in rodeo since he was fourteen or so, and most of the events were competitive versions of usual activities on the ranch. And it turned out, where he was only a decent hockey player, he was a darn good cowboy. Good enough to get him scholarship offers to some decent rodeo programs, should he have wanted it.

But Ford had been itching to get out of Montana when he'd finished high school. Just like Darren was anxious to take over the ranch, Ford had been anxious to get the restless energy and frustrations out of his system. So he'd gone out to a small community college in the heart of Texas, mostly to do something with himself and give him time to figure things out, and it had changed his life.

His rodeo career had taken off from there, and now he was arguably one of the best steer wrestlers on the circuit.

Or so he'd read.

It provided well for him, gave him a nice nest egg tucked away for when he did figure things out, but he was content to continue on the circuit for now. As long as he could do so, he'd keep doing it.

His friends on the Lost Creek circuit were of the same mind, and riding with them was as good as when they'd been on the same team in their college days. Better, in fact, since they were now earning money off of it.

Well, Ryan Prosper wasn't; he'd been forced into

retirement by a nasty injury that put his career in jeopardy if he continued to ride.

But the rest of the gang was still on the circuit. Ryan was now their host in Lost Creek and had settled into an unofficial capacity of running the rodeo events there.

It was about time he'd jumped back in, but Ford got it. He wasn't sure how he'd react when he was no longer able to compete, especially if he wasn't ready to do so. Considering how he avoided pretty much everything else in his personal life, Ford probably would have turned into a complete hermit in some random corner of the country.

At least Ryan had taken over managing his family ranch, and that was no mean feat. His sister, Kellie, brought in additional income to the place by hosting a therapeutic women's retreat or some such out of the homestead house, applying her psychologist training with her ranch upbringing. Broken Hearts Ranch had become a home away from home for several women who'd come seeking exactly what Kellie offered.

It had become a home away from home for Ford and the other guys as well, but in a much different respect.

He was expected there by the end of the week, in fact, to get some practice in before the next events in the area. But he'd been due to come home and check in, so come home he had.

"Wool gathering, bro?"

Ford smirked and glanced up at his big brother. "A little."

Darren laughed to himself. "You're ready to leave, huh?"

He winced. "Is it that obvious?"

"Only if you're looked in the face."

"Don't tell Mom," Ford begged, shifting in his chair and craning his neck. "She'll just fuss and imagine there are problems in the family."

"Well, that's what happens when you're the only one who

leaves." Darren shrugged, not seeming particularly concerned by the idea. "Carly and Shay both stayed local, and Tuck's building his own place on the land. You're the roamer."

Ford raised a brow, suddenly feeling tense where he sat. "Is that a problem?"

Darren shook his head, evenly meeting his gaze. "Nope. I get it. You and I both know we're good, and you know we're all proud of your success." He paused, cocking his head. "You do know that, right?"

"Of course," Ford muttered awkwardly. He ground his teeth a little, shaking his head. "I gotta find where I fit, Darren. You've got your plans, and I don't have any."

"You're gonna need to hold still for five minutes if you want plans," his brother pointed out. "And I'm not talking about a week-and-a-half every four months when you're up here pretending you're helping me out."

Ford grinned, relaxing almost completely now. "So that's obvious, too?"

"Yep." Darren shared a knowing smile. "You're biting your tongue after about day four, just dying to tell me how it could be better and what you would do. Or to tell me off for being bossy."

"That's nothing special. I've been doing that since we were kids."

"You were born telling me to shut up. I know—I remember."

Ford only shrugged. He and Darren were close in age, almost exactly a year apart, and it usually worked in their favor, but it also had put them in frequent competition with each other.

Luckily, they rarely fought.

Anymore.

"You've got it set here," Ford told his brother, knocking

his knuckles against the top of the desk. "You really do. The moment Dad lets up, you're ready to step in, and everything is just going to explode into greatness and fall into place. I'll admit, I'm jealous."

Darren snorted softly. "Jealous. Of waiting for our dad to decide he's old before I can actually do my job the way I want?"

"Of knowing what you want," Ford corrected. "And having it in front of you."

"You know what you want, too," Darren reminded him. "You've just got to figure out where it is." He smiled ruefully, his eyes showing their usual mischievous glint. "And you've gotta be tired enough of rodeo to do something about it."

That was a fair point, but it wasn't about to happen anytime soon.

He'd ride rodeo until he could no longer get on his horse unassisted.

Maybe that should be his plan, then.

Rodeo or die.

"Then I guess I'm not ready," Ford admitted without shame, folding his arms over his loose flannel and shrugging again. "Rodeo still fills the tank for me."

"Glad to hear it. I've got a hundred bucks riding on you in Lost Creek, so don't screw it up."

And that was how things usually went with Darren. His number one fan, just as much as he drove him crazy. Darren wanted Ford out of his hair as much as he wanted his help. Wanted Ford to help make the ranch part of a family dynasty in the area as much as he wanted him to stay in the rodeo world and make a name for himself.

After all, Ford Hopkins from Montana just *had* to be related to the ones who ran the Hopkins Family Ranch, and the fans of rodeo who were potential business partners liked the connection.

Maybe sticking to the circuit as long as he could would be the best way to help his family after all.

There was an idea . . .

"Have you talked to Dad about updating the logo?" Ford asked with a sly smile. "I know you've had Carly working up ideas for ages, but have you seriously done anything with that?"

Darren seemed surprised by the question, probably because he and Ford had never discussed this. It was Carly who had let him in on it. Their older sister couldn't keep a secret to save her life, and she called Ford once a week to blab about whatever came up.

She was a talented graphic designer, working out of her home now, and she'd told Ford more than once that she was dying to actually rebrand the ranch. All she needed was for Darren to give her the green light.

"No," his brother admitted, grumbling as he looked away. "He'll just think I'm trying to take over before my time, and we'll have a fight, which will make Mom cry . . ."

"When you're done predicting the future and whining about it," Ford grunted, "consider suggesting it. Show him whatever Carly's worked up. Dad's a sap—he'll love that it's work in the family."

"Okay . . ." Darren said slowly, eying Ford curiously. "And why the sudden interest in our logo?"

Ford grinned, then gestured at himself. "Because there's a perfectly good canvas here for some free advertising, and you're always saying I should pull my weight for the family. How about I pull some cameras and attention instead?"

Chapter 2

"Did you want an A1C ordered for that patient as well, Dr. Kershaw? It's been two months since her last one, and the numbers weren't great then."

No, Brynn did not want an A1C. She wanted exactly what she had written down on the patient's orders and nothing more. If she had wanted an A1C, she would have written an A1C. The patient wasn't here for her diabetes, she was here for her thyroid. The diabetes appointments were spaced apart the way they were on purpose, and she was *not* about to cross over. Not when the patient had taken thirty minutes to have a three-minute conversation about why she hadn't done anything they had discussed at her last appointment.

Why couldn't people just do what she asked? Was that really so hard? Did she have to do all of the thinking *and* all of the doing here? What was the point of becoming a doctor if she had to do all of the office work, too? Maybe they would like her to walk the patients back to the room herself, draw the blood, do the therapy, submit the billing, and fit them for glasses as well. Why not just hire one person to do everything and save everyone the trouble and money of a whole staff? If only one brain needed to work, what was the point of twelve?

Brynn Kershaw exhaled silently and very slowly, pressing her teeth together until her jaw ached, professional smile perfectly in place as she pretended to consider the idea. "Not this time, Katie. She'll be back in another few weeks, and we can take care of it then."

Her always capable and unfailingly awesome medical assistant, who had no idea what volcano had nearly erupted, nodded and turned away from the office, back toward the patient rooms, leaving Brynn alone once more.

She closed her eyes and released the clenched fists she'd hidden beneath her desk, her nails digging into her palms until the pain of them shot into her wrists. She splayed her suddenly shaking fingers, turning her palms up to see the line of deep indentations in them. Her face flamed with guilt and shame as the fire died down.

Why? Why did the simple question set her off? Why did it send her through the roof? She'd always asked her assistants and nurses to keep their eyes on things like that for the patients, to use their training for critical thinking, not just to do as she asked in complete obedience. Katie was doing exactly what Brynn had always asked of her, and Brynn had wanted to throw something across the room at her. Right at her face.

It made no sense, but these feelings never did.

They never made one bit of sense.

She swallowed and pressed the inside of her wrist against her damp brow, inhaling shakily. They'd just finished with her last patient of the day, which was probably why she'd lost it. These surges, or whatever they were, always came at the end of the day.

Or when she was stressed.

Which wasn't always at the end of the day.

But that was it for her day. She didn't need to finish her notes here; she could do those on her laptop at home. If she was going to be surging, she needed to be away from people to do it. She hadn't actually lost it on a coworker or colleague yet, and certainly not on anyone who worked for her, and she did not want to start now.

Her family and friends, on the other hand . . .

Well, they saw her after the end of her workday, when she was at her most stressed. She had much less control then.

She should have been able to bite her tongue with the people who loved her best, but somehow, she'd lost whatever filter normal people had in the last year.

Since the truth about Minimus came to light.

Brynn's face suddenly flamed, her heart rate picking up, galloping furiously against her temples, her wrists, and the soles of her feet. A glower took over her features, and she felt almost sick with the sudden rise in emotions.

No, she told herself. *No. This has to stop.*

She waited, trying some deep breathing, picking a spot on the wall and focusing on it, counting backwards from seven—everything she had seen when she'd been scrolling on her phone at two in the morning last week. It should have worked, one or all.

But nothing was happening.

Except her anger growing hotter.

She'd scream herself into a frenzy in about ten minutes if this didn't back down. She knew that for sure; two weeks ago, she'd had to grab a pillow from a patient room to do so and had almost passed out from it.

She refused to do that again. He could not have this much power anymore. That was why she'd given him that name. Minimus was tiny and insignificant, a weakling attempt at a gladiator that would get eaten alive in three seconds flat. He had no real name.

Not anymore.

And he would *not* continue to rile her up just by existing.

Pressing her back teeth together again, Brynn turned to her computer and signed out before swinging her chair around to pick up her purse. She hurried out of her office, turning down the back hallway to avoid seeing any of the office staff or lingering patients who might think of new questions or use the dreaded phrase, "While I am here."

Nothing set her off like those words.

But she hadn't liked them much before the Minimus incident, so there was that.

"Brynn!"

She jerked to a stop, hissing to herself in the weakest attempt at self-soothing known to man. She took two careful steps back and smiled into the office of her colleague. "Hey, Craig."

Craig was a classic in this office—mid-fifties, still ran marathons, had a sense of humor, spent enough time with his patients to keep them happy but not enough to get trapped, and had a gift with babies. He was also observant to a fault and loved to pry. His wife commented on it at every office party and staff dinner.

He'd know if she were about to go off.

He sat back in his chair, grinning at the end of the workday like he was living the dream. "You're racing out of here. Got a date?"

"Yes," she told him in a complete deadpan. "With Netflix, Ben, and Jerry."

He chuckled and picked up a stress ball from his desk, tossing it from one hand to the other. "It's a gorgeous day out. You should get out there. Go for a walk, a run, a ride. Soak up some sun."

"Are you telling me to be more active?" Brynn asked with a tilt of her head. "Or to get more vitamin D?"

"Whatever it is that will get you back on your game."

She gritted her teeth against the rise of defenses. "I don't have seasonal affective disorder in June in New Mexico, Craig. And I walk three miles every morning plus do free weights every other day."

"Cut out carbs?"

"Only if you want me to go postal on this place."

"Had a mono test recently?"

"I have all the energy I need."

"What about your sugars? Let me order you an A1C for kicks."

"Craig," Brynn ground out, not bothering to hide her irritation now. "I see Meghan for my primary care. What exactly do you think is wrong with me?"

The man might have been invasive, but he was no fool. He straightened in his chair and held up his hands. "Hey, I didn't say a thing was wrong. You're pulling great numbers, and you've barely missed a step. You just seem a little . . . I don't know, off or something. I'd say tired, except you're right, you have energy. I'd say anxious, but you're keeping pretty cool. I'd say depressed, but . . ."

"The point?" Brynn interrupted, folding her arms, ignoring the urge to laugh at his claim that she was keeping cool.

She was anything but cool these days.

"Something's up," Craig said bluntly, giving her a sympathetic smile. "I can see it. Don't know what, exactly, but you don't have to be a genius or a gossip to have an idea. If you want to talk, the door's always open."

Brynn blinked at the offer, some snarling, three-headed dog within her straining at the leash containing it. "I got a divorce, Craig. Not a disease, not a disorder. And despite what anyone thinks, I'm not a robot. I'm dealing." She exhaled shortly and forced herself to try for a smile. "Thanks for the concern."

"And butt out?" He grinned, nodding at the implied answer. "Can do. Just remember what I said about the door."

"Got it." Brynn nodded back and turned back down the hall, the snarling dog now all-out barking within her chest. She skipped the elevator and thundered her way down the back stairs instead, grateful she'd been smart enough to wear sturdy flats today instead of her nicer shoes that would have risked her rolling an ankle or tripping and breaking something.

Breathing almost frantically, she shoved at the door to the parking lot and made a beeline for her car, fumbling with the keys in her purse and struggling to find the unlock button, accidentally pressing the alarm first. The blaring shot her pulse through the roof, and her eyes began to flood with tears she couldn't explain as she crammed her thumb against the unlock button. She yanked at the door handle and practically threw herself inside the car, tossing her bag on the passenger seat and slamming the door shut as fast as she could.

Then she sat.

Tears rolled down her cheeks as her labored breathing suddenly took on sounds, some growling sob that rumbled its way up her chest on each exhale, turning to a wheeze on the inhale. Her hands became fists again, and those fists pressed into her eyes hard as her body shook with the strained symphony currently wracking her. A hoarse yelling began then, roaring into a fury at herself, at her life, at Minimus, at every surge that had lit her up that day and could only now be released, and she would not be content with just one.

She yelled again, and again, and again, her head beginning to ache with the force of each one, and the air required to give them that force. Then she whimpered weakly as it all left her, taking with it all the energy and strength she'd relied on for the day. She rested her head on the steering wheel, folding her arms across her stomach, as there was nothing left but tears.

What was wrong with her? Where had her stability and control gone? Where had her happiness and humor and hope gone?

Was she going crazy?

She wasn't the only person she knew who'd gotten a divorce. She wasn't even the only person in her family. But none of them had developed a hair trigger on a pile of dynamite. None of them had screamed themself hoarse in their car without a specific reason.

None of them had gone crazy.

Why could she not have coped by indulging in takeout and ice cream? Twenty pounds would be a cakewalk compared to this insanity. She'd turn into Craig's running partner and take care of that.

But this?

She'd need to start walking between patients soon just to get her surges under control. Yoga at lunch. Whale sounds when sitting at her desk. Chocolate around the clock.

Well, she already did that, and it just made her less hangry.

Didn't do anything about her surges.

Head pounding, eyes burning, Brynn inhaled slowly, and exhaled slowly, then sat up and checked her surroundings. No one around, no one to see. It was why she parked in the back, away from physician parking, away from patient parking.

Just . . . away.

Sniffling, she checked her phone, sighing at the message notification.

"Please don't be from work," she whispered to her car as she tapped the app.

She managed a smile as she saw her best friend's name across the top.

Kennedy wants to see Auntie Brynn. Aaron is working late. Can we swing by with a pizza?

Cute goddaughter and free pizza? Maybe that would be the cure to volcano days.

She texted back quickly. *Yes. Please. I'll be home in fifteen.*

The drive home was simple enough, even with traffic, and the heat of the day had little effect on her. Albuquerque had been home for six years now, and she hadn't been bothered by the heat of it even once. Coming from Missouri, she was used to heat and humidity, but doing her residency in Arizona had opened her eyes to the glories of dry heat, and she was perfectly content to stay here forever. Her family was all over the country at this point, and even her parents weren't in Missouri anymore.

A cross-country family, so to speak.

She had met Mandi shortly after she moved to Albuquerque with Minimus, and they'd connected at a company social for the airline Minimus and Mandi's husband, Aaron, flew for. The men hadn't really clicked, but Mandi and Brynn had been inseparable from then on.

When Brynn had been named godmother for their daughter, Kennedy, her life had brightened notably, considering the crap show it had been for that entire year. Rumors had been everywhere, but Minimus hadn't said anything. Even when confronted, he hadn't said a thing.

Baby Kennedy had given Brynn a reprieve from her growing misery.

Now she was a jabbering eighteen-month-old, and her

sweet obsession with hugs was going to be exactly what Brynn needed.

Her condo was as neat and tidy as she left it, which meant she wouldn't have to do any rapid cleanup before they got here. Just a few adjustments to make sure the place was Kennedy-proof, and she was good to go. Next step was to get out of the faux-fancy trousers she'd worn for the day, which were really yoga pants with a crease, and the sweats and oversized tee were as good as a warm blanket on a cold night after the day she'd had.

She always spent her free time in sweats and an oversized tee these days, but it felt especially good at the moment.

A very childish knock sounded at her door, and Brynn grinned at it, her energy spiking in a way she could have used hours ago. "Who could that be at my door?" she asked loudly. "I just don't know."

Her favorite giggles met her ears, and she opened the door to see the most adorable white-blonde pigtails and blue eyes known to man. And she was grinning at Brynn like she was the sun.

"Kennedy!" Brynn squealed as though this was a surprise, reaching her arms out. "Come see me!"

The little girl leaned for her, and immediately hugged her neck.

Brynn cradled Kennedy against her, breathing in the sweet scent of baby wash, grass, and apple juice as though it were the greatest perfume in the world. "Hi, sweet baby. Auntie Brynn needed her Kennedy tonight."

"Any Bin," Kennedy said, patting Brynn's shoulders and giggling to herself.

"Where's Mama?" Brynn asked her, frowning. "Where'd Mama go?"

Kennedy twisted in her arms and pointed at her equally blonde mother. "Mama dere."

Brynn gasped as Mandi reacted to the identification, and held up the box of pizza.

"Mama's here," Mandi agreed in a singsong voice, "and she's got dinner!"

"Then Mama can come in," Bryn replied in kind, stepping back.

Mandi entered the condo, kicking off her shoes and dropping the diaper bag slung over her shoulder before shutting the door. "Good, I'm glad Brynn is having dinner with me tonight. I was a little worried it would be cranky Brynn again, which is why I went for pizza instead of Chinese."

Brynn scowled at her as they moved into the kitchen. "I'm never cranky with you."

"Uh, okay." Mandi widened her eyes, snorting to herself as she set the pizza on the counter and pulled plates from the cabinets.

"I'm not!" Brynn insisted while Kennedy played with the still-curled ends of her hair.

Mandi pressed her hands onto the counter and gave her a hard look. "Honey. Last week, you bit my head off for doing your dishes, and you ripped into Aaron for not taking the jump seat back from L.A. a day earlier. Which, I might add, does not directly affect you. You told me not to be your mother when I asked how you were doing on Sunday, and you stormed to your room like an angry teenager when I asked if that was a hole in your sweats. I love you, Brynn. You're the sister I never had. And because of that, I gotta tell you that you're this close to having another name entirely, and it starts with the same letter." She nodded firmly and went back to getting the pizza out.

Brynn sank slowly onto her couch, letting Kennedy wriggle out of her hold to the floor. "Am I really?"

"Do you want me to be truthful or supportive?" Mandi asked her, glancing up. "Because the answer is yes, but it's not going to ruin our friendship. Toolbox did you rotten, and I hope he gets a disease, so you get some kind of a pass there."

"Minimus," Brynn murmured with a swallow. "I named him Minimus. It was the most insignificant medical term I could think of."

Mandi paused with two plates in hand, considering that. "I like it. I'd probably have chosen a cancer of some kind, but I like insignificance, too." She came over and handed Brynn a plate. "You look like you haven't slept in three days. Is that just from today?"

Brynn nodded, picking up her pizza and taking a bite. "I've been told I look like something's wrong."

"You do," her friend said bluntly. "And you act like it, too, which fits, because something *is* wrong, and his name is—"

"Don't say it," Brynn snapped with a warning look. "This is a him-free zone in every respect."

Mandi held up her hands. "Sorry, okay." She frowned a little, and turned more toward Brynn. "This can't go on, sweetie. Can you take some time off? Get away for a while? The divorce is done, so you really are free. Go rejuvenate somewhere. Or do a staycation. Maybe see someone . . ."

"Therapy?" Brynn shook her head firmly. "I'm fine, Mandi. Really. Just exhausted."

"You're always fine, and it's never the truth." Mandi pursed her lips in thought. "Tell you what. I'm going to start researching and plotting. I was a travel agent once upon a time, so let me build you a few options. When you're ready, or you're about to lose your marbles, I'll send them to you. Because if that other Brynn sticks around much longer, this is not going to be optional, okay?"

"I'm *fine*," Brynn insisted.

Mandi shook her head, taking a bite of pizza. "Say it one more time—you might get an echo. This is happening. You just tell me when it is."

Brynn rolled her eyes and sank back against her couch. There was no arguing with Mandi when she got like this. Besides, a vacation could be nice. "Okay. I'll tell you when. Bossy."

"Another 'b' word." Mandi announced, settling in comfortably. "We're on a roll."

CHAPTER 3

FORD ROLLED DOWN THE windows of his truck as he crossed the state line into Texas, breathing in the air deeply. It was like sticking his head under a hand dryer in a public restroom, but there was something salty and earthy about this air, and it ruffled his hair with the wild, dirty fingers that reminded him of rodeo.

How could the Texas air take him back to the arena?

His mind began to spin on the rodeos he was missing on the circuit right now. He and the other guys in the Original Six had committed to competing at the annual rodeo set at the Lost Creek Days festival, along with some other decent names on the circuit right now, but doing so meant he was going to miss some good competition. It was probably worth it, all in all, giving back to the town that had given him so much over the years.

But there was something about competing that was just satisfying for him. He wasn't one of the hotshots, and he had a good rapport with every other cowboy he had gone up against, but once that steer came out of the chute, a switch clicked over within him. He could outride anyone else there, and wrestle the steer to the ground before half of the others could have even grabbed the horns. He owned that event every time he rode, and it never got old.

The glory tended to go to the rough stock riders—bareback, saddle bronc, and bull riders—but there was something special about steer wrestling. An underappreciation that made every one of them an underdog clawing for respect in the rodeo world.

Ford demanded that respect, and, more often than not, it came.

Once that buzzer sounded, though, and he stepped out of the limelight, he was back to just riding along and minding his own business. It was a helluva way to make a living, but he loved it. Last season, he had made more money than ever, and he was shaping up to be even better this year. Time would tell, and if he could break three-and-a-half seconds this season . . .

Well, that would turn a few heads, wouldn't it?

He grinned and glanced over at his driving companion, currently sticking his massive head between the driver and passenger seats, silently navigating the drive and drooling all over Ford's center console.

"You getting antsy, boy?" he asked the dark, hulking mastiff. "You've been to Texas before. Does it look familiar?"

Sherlock suddenly lolled his tongue out of his mouth, panting his humid, rank breath in Ford's face.

"You're worse than Lars," Ford grumbled, gently pushing the dog's face away from his own. "It's not *that* hot."

A tinny version of a Johnny Cash song sounded in his truck, and he glanced at his phone, hooked on a stand in one of the vents. He grinned at the caller ID and pressed accept. "Marty. You enjoying your rest and relaxation?"

"Not particularly, no," his partner reported, sounding a little strained and not in his usual joking mood.

"What's up?" Ford asked immediately. "Kids too much?"

He heard the man exhale roughly. "I don't know how to tell you this, pal, but I busted my leg up pretty bad working on my father-in-law's combine. Had surgery this morning, and I'm out of commission for three months minimum."

Ford swore under his breath. "Sorry to hear that, bud. You sound good for just being cut up."

"I'm on the good meds, and I'm taking a nap when we hang up, so I'm great," Marty said with a laugh. "I just feel bad I'm leaving you high and dry, especially when you're on this kind of roll."

"I can find me a stand-in hazer, don't you worry," Ford assured him, forcing a note of confidence into his tone that he didn't feel.

"But not one that's been riding with you for three years."

That was true, but Ford wasn't about to give his partner any guilt for something that wasn't his fault.

"Any cowboy worth his salt can drive a steer for me," Ford reiterated. "I'll talk to the Six and try 'em out down in Lost Creek. Maybe I'll like it better than dealing with your smart mouth all the time."

"Your boys wouldn't know a flank from a flag, but good luck with that."

He heard Marty sigh, and knew it was just killing the guy to be out of commission for a while, least of all because of the lurch it would leave Ford in.

But it wasn't that bad; any capable cowboy could guide a steer like a hazer—it was just the timing that needed to be worked out. He knew plenty of cowboys with rodeo experience, and he'd find someone to stand in for Marty.

This was not a problem.

He refused to let it be.

"You heal up," Ford told him. "Don't worry about me. No guilt, got it?"

"Not likely."

"Then just don't tell me about your guilt, okay? Cuz we're good."

Marty signed off with a laugh, and Ford hung up, his smile fading as he drove the wide-open Texas highway.

"Crap, Sherlock," he muttered to the dog beside him. "Crap, crap, crap."

Finding someone on short notice who could pick up Ford's style might be harder than he let on. Even among the Six, he wasn't sure how it would go. They were his best bet, hands down, and they could practice in Lost Creek easily enough, but he might have to adjust his expectations for this rodeo.

Lost Creek Days wasn't one of the major events of the summer, so there was that. It was a tribute to the town, their heritage festival, and he went back when he could, to pay homage to the place that had done so much and meant so much to him. He could afford to find his new hazer there without sacrificing this season as a whole, and they'd just make it work.

That was it. Easy enough.

Ford sputtered his lips as he went over various options in his head, each without experience in the last few years, though they'd certainly practiced enough back in the day. But for three years, it had only been Marty, because they worked so well together.

Finding someone else for the rest of the season wasn't going to be fun.

One step at a time, he reminded himself. Lost Creek and the Six would have his back, and they'd figure something out.

He turned up his radio and began beating a rhythm on his steering wheel in time with the song, whistling the melody. He couldn't even bring himself to be all that stressed about his situation at the moment. Not when the Texas sky hung above him and the land stretched out so brightly before him. He was a Montana boy, but man, did his heart sure adore Texas.

Maybe this was the place he could fit for the future. Maybe there was something to that feeling he got each time when he came back.

It was almost like being home.

Without all the siblings and stress and itching to be away.

Ford loved his family. He just needed to feel like his life had a direction, like the rest of theirs did.

Maybe Texas could give that to him.

His mind became a hum of images and thoughts without much by way of context or theme, that blank openness that came with autopilot driving on wide-open highways. Words from songs would filter through, and he would absently sing along if he knew the words, maybe finger an imaginary guitar once he figured out the chords and notes.

Music was a family tradition, though he could fairly safely say he was the most musically-inclined of his siblings. Not the most talented, necessarily, but most inclined.

They made a pretty fair band when they were all together.

It had been a while since they'd played together. They should have done that while he was home.

He blinked as an exit sign caught his attention, his eyes flicking toward it.

Amarillo.

Man, he loved Amarillo. He hadn't stopped in a few hours; he ought to stretch his legs and fill up the truck. Might as well stop at the Cadillac Ranch while he was here.

The place was the pride and joy of Amarillo, in a way. Ten classic Cadillac cars sticking out of the ground, noses buried in the dirt, and it was called art. He'd been to other parts of Amarillo several times over the years, but he'd only been to that place once.

Ford checked the clock on his dashboard, shrugging to himself. There was plenty of time to get down to Lost Creek before his first practice tomorrow. Late night, but if he got tired, he'd pull off and sleep. He'd done that last night somewhere after Colorado Springs, and he did it when he was on the circuit driving from place to place.

Might as well enjoy the drive he was taking and the beauty of the country he was so proud to be part of.

He took the next exit, whistling to himself as he looked for signs for the Cadillac Ranch. He could have pulled it up on his phone, he supposed, but where was the fun in that?

His phone began to ding and buzz in its holder, and he glanced at the screen.

The Chute was on a roll, it seemed. His friends in the Original Six had started a group text, and someone had named it The Chute, which made Ford wonder if they were cowboys or steers in the scenario. Whichever it was, the thread was always full of hot air and an excessive use of GIFs.

He couldn't tell who had said what, or what the current stupidity was, but he'd have to check in pretty soon. There was nothing worse than not joining in when the guys were on a roll. The latecomer was automatically targeted, and it could get ugly.

Lars was still cranky about his turn last week.

Pulling into a gas station at a truck stop, Ford climbed out and started filling up the truck.

"No, Sherlock," he told the suddenly whining dog. "Not here. You can get out in a bit, but not here." He stretched out his back, picked up trash and clutter in the truck, then leaned against it while he waited for the pump to finish.

"Hey! You're Ford Hopkins, ain't ya?"

Ford smiled at the older man on the other side of the pump and tapped the brim of his cowboy hat. "Yes, sir."

The man wheezed a cackle and hooked his thumbs into his worn and faded belt. "Shoot, boy, I saw you down in Lubbock last year. You rastled that bull down afore I had a chance to sip my beer! Clean as a whistle, and those hooves up in the air like one of them piñatas. You comin' back round here soon?"

"I think so," Ford hedged as he glanced at the numbers on the pump, waiting for it to reach a full tank. "We're in Lost Creek next weekend, but after that, we've got a few gigs in quick succession."

"Ted! It's Ford Hopkins! That Montana kid who wrestles the steers in the rodeo! 'Member that?" his fan called to some companion of his that Ford couldn't see.

Ford bit back a sigh, suddenly wishing he had kept going on his drive.

"He's the only Montana kid I remember in the rodeo!" the man barked with some irritation. "I don't care what you say, I'm gonna see if he wants to come with us to the Cadillac Ranch, swap some rodeo stories or something."

Well, there went those plans.

"Ford, you got plans today?" his fan asked as he stuck his head back around the pump.

"Yes, sir," Ford told him at once, keeping his tone apologetic as he set the nozzle back on the pump. "I'm expected down in Lost Creek. I've only stopped over to fill up the truck."

"Aw, shoot." The old man grinned, his few teeth making an appearance. "Can I talk you into a meal? Bit of small talk?"

Ford winced as he closed the gas tank. "Wish I could, sir. I'm on a pretty tight deadline. It was a real pleasure to meet you, though. Thanks for callin' out."

The guy nodded, tipping his straw hat at him. "Sure thing, son. You keep doing your thing with them steers."

"Yes, sir." Ford nodded and moved back around to his door, sliding back into the truck and turning it on as quickly as he could. He pulled around to get back on the main road before he'd even buckled his seat belt.

He didn't need to go see cars in the ground anyway. It was cool, but he'd wanted to go by himself, not with a couple of old cusses who wouldn't leave him alone. He wasn't in rodeo for the fame, and he never minded flying under the radar. Direct attention outside of the arena made him uncomfortable, and he'd go to great lengths to avoid it.

Except for music. He'd play at bars or around a campfire or in someone's home if asked, but those scenes didn't lead to all that much attention after he finished.

That was the distinction.

He pulled over and hooked Sherlock's leash to his collar, flipping on the hazard lights as he got out to let the dog relieve himself in some brush before the next leg.

"Come on, boy," he said, opening the passenger door and bringing the seat forward to let him in the back. "How's the water situation?" He looked at the travel bowl and grunted. "Parched, huh? You shoulda said." He reached for a bottle of water and emptied it into the bowl, then readjusted the seat, shut the door, and went back around to his own side to climb back in.

A minute or so later, he was back on the interstate, shaking his head to himself, when his phone rang. Glancing at the screen, he grunted in surprise before pushing the button. "Bulldogger, what's up?"

"Hey there," Ryan Prosper's voice sounded through the truck's speakers. "You gettin' in today?"

"That's the plan," Ford replied with a sigh. "We'll see if it sticks."

"Where are you now?"

"Amarillo." He merged into traffic, trying to look ahead to the next sign. "I'm about to the city limits, I think."

Ryan said something to someone else, his words not clear to Ford. "You up for a detour?"

Ford laughed once. "Depends what it is. Am I getting hotcakes the size of a manhole cover wherever I'm going?"

"You could probably finagle a way to get those, but that's not what I had in mind. There's a pecan farm just outside of Fort Worth, and Kells wants to know if you'd drive over there and pick up a few bushels."

"That would depend." Ford smiled a little, though no one would see it. "What do I get out of the favor?"

There was a little scuffling, and then a new voice came on. "Ford," Kellie said firmly, "you bring me those pecans before noon tomorrow, and I'll bake you the first pie with them."

Ford grinned, now laughing fully in the cabin of the truck. "It's a lotta pecans for one lonely pie, Kells."

"We're teaching the ladies how to do pecan pie," Kellie told him with her infinite patience, though there was a teasing note to her voice, as usual. "And then Mariah's going to sell the ones that turn out well enough. I promise I will bake you a perfect pecan pie all for yourself."

"Uh-huh, sounds promising. What about the pies that don't turn out well enough to sell at Mariah's?"

He heard a less-than-patient sigh on the other side of the line. "If they are safe enough to eat, Ford, you can have the ones that don't turn out, too. Happy?"

"Very," he said with a nod. "Text me the address, and I'll swing by and get them. Do they know I'm coming?"

"They will; I'll call them next. Thank you so much, Ford. This is a lifesaver."

"Well, I do live my life to look better than Ryan," he assured her. "Just add this to the list."

"Got it. One more and I can officially switch you two out."

"Hey!" Ryan called from somewhere in the background. Sounds of scuffling ensued, and then Ryan was back on. "Whatever, dude. Don't feel like you need to get here tonight now that we're adding time to your drive."

"I'll do it, no big deal. Care if I bunk out on your couch when I get in?"

"You know where the key is. Thanks for doing this, man."

Ford scoffed, sputtering softly. "I'm getting my favorite pie out of the deal. This is purely selfish."

"Right. Thanks for nothing, then."

"Sounds about right." Sherlock shoved his wrinkled face up against Ford's shoulder and started surveying their route, way closer to Ford than before. "Hey, back off, Sherlock!"

"Sherlock's with you?" Ryan laughed in delight. "Sherlock!" He began a bad impersonation of the dog's rarely heard bark, a deep, rasping sort of howl that was really awful.

Sherlock groaned and whined at hearing it.

"Yeah, that about sums it up, doesn't it?" Ford replied, then he straightened in his seat, remembering what he would need when he got to Lost Creek. "Hey, Ryan . . . My hazer's injured and out for a while. Can you round up some guys for me to practice with there? I need to find someone before showtime."

"Shoot. Yeah, no worries, bro. I'll get some guys together. Worse comes to worse, I'll do it. If I remember how."

Ford smiled at that. If Ryan Prosper forgot anything about rodeo, even the smallest detail, Ford would gnaw on his own boots.

"You'll remember. Thanks, man. See you when I see you."

He hung up, ideas spinning back and forth in his mind. It might be easier than he thought to get a new hazer lined up.

Ryan Prosper could probably do the job as well as Marty did it, if not better.

This could be very interesting after all. Very.

Chapter 4

"Thank you, Doctor. I know I can be a worrier sometimes, and I really appreciate your time."

Brynn smiled at her anxious patient, rubbing her arm. "Of course, Mrs. Pike. That's what I'm here for. Laney at the desk there will take care of that referral and the orders, okay?" Brynn nodded and gently nudged Mrs. Pike in that direction.

The kind woman waved and headed that way, leaving Brynn there to look over the charts of the next patient room.

Except she wasn't reading anything.

Couldn't.

She was behind in her schedule now. Really behind. Mrs. Pike hadn't just worried in that room—she'd unpacked every ounce of baggage she'd stored up. Everything she had read online about what she suspected, everything she attributed to this disease or that, everything that had kept her up at night.

There had been no getting around any of it, and Brynn had always been able to calm those sorts of patients. It was part of the job, and similar patients came every week, if not every day. She always had a full schedule, and there were a lot of issues that patients needed to discuss with her. Every day, she would go through concerns with patients. That was what she did.

Today, it was too much.

Why had she let Mrs. Pike ramble? Why hadn't she cut her off? Why not tell her that obsessing over her possible health conditions was a sign of other issues entirely? Why not tell her she did not have time to discuss everything and to pick two things?

It would have let Brynn get caught up. It would have kept her stress from getting this high. It would have spared her ears and her mind.

But she hadn't. She'd let Mrs. Pike talk. Pretended she had all the time in the world.

Because patient care was ingrained in her, and it wasn't Mrs. Pike's fault Brynn's schedule was overcrowded.

It was a miracle she hadn't actually yelled at the woman.

"Dr. Kershaw, there's a call for you from Radiology."

Brynn blinked, trying to focus. "Is it urgent?" she asked whoever had told her. "I've got patients."

"I'll check and get a number for you to call back."

"Thank you."

"Dr. Kershaw, can you sign this please?" One of the receptionists stepped forward, a medication refill request in hand.

Brynn glossed over it, forcing herself to see and comprehend. "That's just a request for a ninety-day supply. That's fine." She signed it quickly, nodding at the woman.

"Dr. Kershaw?"

Would they not shut up? Could they not see that she was working? Why couldn't they just wait until she was done with patients?

"Yes?" she asked, her tone clipped, but not angry, thank goodness.

"Mrs. Tyler wanted you to know the dose pack didn't work."

"Refer to orthopedics," Brynn whispered. She swallowed hard. "I'll . . . put the referral in at lunch."

"I'll tell her, thank you."

Brynn nodded, a faint humming starting in her ears.

Everyone needed to shut up. Stop talking to her. Stop saying her name.

"Dr. Kershaw."

"Dr. Kershaw?"

"Hey, Dr. Kershaw . . ."

The words on the chart before her trembled in her hands as she tried to prepare, tried to gather herself.

Discussion of lab results. She'd already decided on a course here. Samples.

Great.

Inhale. Exhale. Inhale. Exhale.

She knocked on the door in front of her before she could stop herself. "Hi, Mr. Walsh. Let's talk about these labs." She sat on the stool in the room, took one look at the man, then stood up and turned to the computer, his expression telling her he had a lot on his mind.

She could not do that. She had six more patients to get through, which meant she wouldn't get a lunch, which meant she would be starving before she hit two in the afternoon, and everything was worse when she was hungry . . .

"Your numbers are better than I thought," Brynn announced, glancing over her shoulder at Mr. Walsh with a forced smile as she pulled the data up on the screen. "Not as good as we'd like, but not as bad as we thought. There's a sample of a medication I'd like you to try, and it'll help to keep . . ."

"I'll take whatever you say, Doc," Mr. Walsh interrupted,

as though it was helpful. "I can't keep track of them all anyway, but I take 'em every day."

Brynn had started to nod, the irritation of being interrupted making her bristle, when his words processed. "Every day?" she repeated.

Mr. Walsh nodded. "Every day, Doc. Every one of 'em."

She turned back to the computer, clicking through a few screens, then biting back a sigh as she looked back at him. "Mr. Walsh. Last month, we discussed that new medication for your rheumatoid arthritis. I told you it only needs to be taken on Monday mornings. One pill on Monday mornings. Do you remember that?"

"I sure do!" He nodded proudly, swinging his legs a little, almost like a child. "You said once a week, and the bottle says to take it on Monday mornings."

"So that's what you've been doing?" Brynn asked.

As she feared, Mr. Walsh shook his head. "No, ma'am. I figured if once a week was good, every day was even better. Once the headaches went away, I felt good as new."

Brynn pressed her teeth together, her jaw aching from the pressure she was applying. "Unfortunately, Mr. Walsh, that is not how this works. I'm going to have to cut this appointment short now so you can go get new labs drawn. Don't take that medication again until you hear from my office."

"Which pills are those?" he asked, his feet pausing in their swinging. "The yellow ones?"

Her teeth clicked as they slid against each other in their grinding, and she pressed her thumbnail into the skin of her middle finger until the sharp pain was almost unbearable. "As your pharmacist will have told you," she said slowly, "the size, shape, and color of your pills will depend on the manufacturer. Why don't you take your pill bottles over to the hospital pharmacy and have them help you out? I'll send a note down that you'll be coming." She nodded, starting toward the door.

"And my samples?"

"They'll be at the desk with your lab orders," Brynn assured him, forcing another smile. "Come on out."

She started down the hall, her pulse thudding in the sides of her neck, her face growing hot. She scribbled down the labs she wanted done and handed the note to Katie. "More labs. And give him samples. And tell the pharmacy he needs help telling his medicines apart."

"Can do," Katie said with a firm nod. "You've got three messages, two of them urgent. Also, Dr. Halliday at the ER would like you to call her at your convenience—something about a patient of yours showing up there with complications."

Brynn started to shake, even as she took the memos. "And how many patients are in rooms still?"

"Four in rooms, last one in the waiting room."

She'd never make it.

Biting down on the inside of her lip, she turned away. "Thank you, Katie."

She heard her assistant greet Mr. Walsh, taking care of his needs, and she passed her office quickly, going to the one two doors down. "Melanie? What's your schedule like right now?"

The nurse practitioner looked up in surprise, but smiled widely. "Just finished. You need me?"

Brynn nodded, swallowing as she felt the shaking within her intensify "I'm so backed up. Could you help with a few patients?"

"Of course!" Melanie was on her feet at once, straightening her white coat and coming around the desk. "Any preference?"

Full Rigged

"Nope, I just need a minute, so if you could jump in . . ." Brynn tightened the clamping of her teeth, which were now chattering freely.

Melanie nodded and patted her arm. "Gotcha. I'm on it." She grinned and moved around her toward the patient rooms with a bounce in her step Brynn hadn't had in a long time.

Releasing a barely contained, unsteady breath, Brynn backtracked to her office as fast as she dared, closing the door behind her.

"No," she groaned low, trailing off into a whimper and squeezing her eyes shut.

"Dr. Kershaw?" someone asked from the other side of the door.

"Just a sec, I need to call the ER back," she replied, somehow making her tone neutral.

The steps retreated, and Brynn immediately put both hands over her mouth.

Then she let go, releasing a roar barely muffled by her palms, curling up against her boiling fury. Her arms and legs seemed to catch fire, and her head pounded at a furious pace. A frantic edge suddenly found its way into her thoughts, and she looked around her office, wide-eyed. She needed to throw something, squeeze something, tear anything and everything.

She needed some actual release to this madness.

The phone at her desk rang, and she turned to it, unable to consider adding one more thing to her plate. She raced around the desk and yanked the cord from the back of the phone, then hurled the phone against the wall with a growling hiss lashing against her clenched teeth, some ounce of sanity reminding her that she was at work and others might hear her. She stared at the remains of the phone on the floor, her chest heaving, ears pounding.

It wasn't enough.

She whirled and knocked everything nearest her off the desk: a cup of pens, her nameplate, reports for the afternoon patients, an office dish of paperclips, and a stapler. All of them crashed to the floor, and none of them gave her relief.

Rage gave way to shame, and shame buckled her knees, sending her limply to the ground, every breath tearing at her lungs and draining her. Then she couldn't control it, gasping and rasping at an inhuman pace, sobbing without tears, her head swimming in air that did nothing for her body. She curled her fingers into the carpet, her nails gripping hard, trying to count to ten, or hold her breath, or ground herself in some way to her present rather than float on the tossing waves of her uncontrolled emotions.

She was going to die here in this office. Amid her mess and her rage, she was going to die. Minimus would get everything he hadn't gotten in the settlement, and he would win. He'd break her, at last.

She didn't want to be broken. Didn't want to be under his thumb. Didn't want . . .

She didn't want this.

She was losing her mind, losing herself, and losing all awareness of life as she had known it or would want to know it.

She needed help.

A lot of help.

She dragged in a long, slow, body-shuddering breath, then released it in a rush. Then she did so again. And again. And again.

Her head stopped swimming and only buzzed painfully as the blood returned to her face and limbs, ears thundering on each pulse. She rolled to her back, bending her knees and setting her feet flat on the floor.

Staring up at the ceiling, her brow growing damp with

belated perspiration, Brynn felt tears trickle from the corners of her eyes down to her ears and into her hair.

"I need help," she whispered to herself. With a swallow, she turned her head and grabbed her phone where it lay on the floor, swept there by her arm in the fury of her surge. She pulled up Mandi's number, then put the phone to her ear.

"What's wrong?" her friend asked in greeting, her voice on alert.

Brynn exhaled very slowly. "I need help, Mandi. Can you find me somewhere to go and get it? Not, like, padded walls, but . . . something away and stress-free?"

"Absolutely. I've got some options lined up. I'll send them to you." She paused, and Brynn could hear the hesitation. "Do I need to come get you?"

"No," Brynn told her, tears choking her would-be strong voice. "But I'd really love it if you could just talk to me for a minute."

"You got it, sweetie. Anything in particular?"

"Anything will do."

A gleeful squealing in the background came through the phone, and Mandi sighed noisily. "Well, that sound was my daughter running into the kitchen stark naked and chasing the dog with her diaper on her head. And today, that is just par for the course. Aaron had the genius idea of leaving his pens out . . ."

CHAPTER 5

"THAT'S IT, THAT'S IT! Nicely done, boys. Woo!"

Ford snorted softly and looked over at his partner. "It's like we've never roped anything before, ain't it?"

Eric Davis, calf roper extraordinaire and all-around pain in the rear, shook his head as he loosened the rope in his hand, the ranch hands undoing the rope around the steer. "Somebody needs to find him a hobby."

"You could say that." Ford thumbed his hat back a little, crossing his arms in front of him to stretch his back. "Lars, go find something to do."

Lars Jackson, the best all-around rodeo man Ford had ever met, spread out his hands in a defensive gesture. "What? I'm just supporting you. Offering advice when you screw up. That sort of thing."

"Well, we didn't screw up," Eric shot back. "Did we, West?"

"Do not drag me into this catfight," Westin Farr called with a wave as he worked at a hinge on the corral nearest them. "I wasn't watching, and if you guys can't rope a steer without screwing up, there are bigger issues."

Full Rigged

It had been like this all day, just picking at each other bit by bit, like each of them were the little brother of the group. Reid hadn't gotten back from D.C. yet, and Ryan actually had work to do on the ranch. Which, come to think of it, was probably what West was helping with at the moment. They hadn't driven out to the rodeo grounds in Lost Creek today, and instead had stayed on Broken Hearts Ranch to practice a little. It wasn't full arena size, but they weren't going full arena speeds either. It was more a way to kill time than anything else, even though they'd asked Ryan what they could do to help today.

He'd been cranky when they'd asked, and said something about surveying before mumbling he'd get back to them.

No texts yet.

The guy might have run away, for all they knew. He loved the land, but there was no denying the amount of work that would be on his plate for the next year or so. A ton of improvements had already been made since he'd officially taken over, but ranch life never ended, and doing more work than the daily expectations could be a challenge.

Which was why it didn't make sense to most of them, least of all Ford, why Ryan wasn't taking advantage of the Six while they were here. Lars was staying in his house, Ford and Eric had just started sleeping in the cabin next to his, and West . . . Well, Westin slept under his truck, for whatever reason, so he didn't really require housing.

Shower facilities, maybe, but not much else.

If worse came to worst, they could just hose him off anyway.

"Ryan? Hey, Ry . . ." Kellie Prosper came around the barn and paused at the sight of them all, scanning around for her brother and frowning when she didn't see him. She propped her hands on her hips and tilted her head, her blonde braid twitching with the motion. "Where is he?"

"Said somethin' about surveying, Kellie," Ford offered from his horse. "Didn't say where."

She scowled at that. "Crap. I forgot about that." She twisted her lips in thought.

"Can we help with something?" Lars offered, turning to her as he leaned on the fence. "We're just killing time here."

Kellie seemed to consider that. "Why not? I've got three guests arriving today, and I just heard from the driver that they've left the airport. Three women for a minimum of thirty days means a lot of physical baggage, so I could use someone to act as a bellhop. Also, I think there's a critter in the attic, and I've got a session starting in twenty. If some of y'all or all y'all could take care of that, and maybe someone go stop Ryan from killing Jake Brady, it would be much appreciated."

"West is good with critters," Ford offered before anyone else could say something. "I'm sure he'll help there."

"Wait, what?" West barked, whirling around again.

Kellie gave him an expectant look. "Something you wanna share there, Westin?"

Ford grinned at his friend, ignoring the snickering Eric on the horse beside him. "You remember, West. You were just telling us about that favorable run-in with a racoon."

West glared at him, shaking his head. "Sure, Kells. I'll take a look in the attic."

Ford was going to regret volunteering him for that task, but he'd take whatever punishment seemed appropriate for this.

"I'll go save Jake from Ryan," Lars volunteered. "I think I know where they're surveying anyway."

"Of course you do," Eric muttered softly.

Ford gave him a quick look. "What?"

Eric leaned closer. "You haven't noticed? Lars is like the new unofficial assistant ranch manager down here. Ryan's got everything in hand, but for some reason, Lars is investing in the place, too."

"Aren't we all?" Ford asked in return. "We've been down here a lot in the last few months, and I know you'd drop everything if Kellie or Ryan needed something here."

"Well, sure, but they're like family, right? Lars is... Lars is something else." Eric shrugged. "Not saying he's wrong. Just saying, he's not the manager, is he?"

Ford knew a little something about stepping in where someone else was in charge, and saw both sides of the question here. "Maybe Ryan appreciates what Lars says about managing the ranch, who knows?"

Eric frowned in thought. "Could be. Hey, Kells? If it's okay, I'm gonna help the boys here get the steers back out to pasture. But Ford's a great bellhop."

"Yeah, he is," Westin agreed quickly, brushing his hands off on his jeans. "Strong, too. Could probably handle all the bags in one trip."

"And give your guests piggyback rides inside at the same time," Lars offered into the stupidity.

Kellie was clearly trying not to laugh as she looked at Ford. "With such accolades, how can I refuse?"

Ever the good sport, despite the turn of his own game, Ford gave her a crooked smile. "You can't. I'll take another pecan pie for my trouble, though."

"You know full well those are long gone," Kellie told him, folding her arms. "And you had plenty."

"Then I'll just presume I'm invited to the homestead for dinner one of these nights." He climbed down from the horse and patted her neck. "Or breakfast. I'll never turn down some of your biscuits and gravy."

Kellie laughed once. "Sunday morning, y'all come on over, and I'll whip some up. And what the hay? We'll do dinner at the homestead either tonight or tomorrow. Lemme take stock of my new guests first, though." Her smile turned softer, her smile less exuberant. "Based on their applications, at least one is pretty skittish around men."

That sobered the entire group, and Ford took a moment before speaking again, coming over to where she waited on the other side of the fence. "Whatever you need, Kells. Whatever *they* need."

She rubbed his arm, smiling up at him. "Thanks, Ford. You guys have been so great with the guests, and I think it's really gone a long way to help so many of them. There's something to be said for good, honest men."

"For everyone else, there's Lars," Ford said without missing a beat.

Lars mimed punching him in the face, and Ford grinned at him while the others laughed. Then Lars turned to Kellie. "Should I take an ATV out there, or . . . ?"

She nodded. "Ryan's got his truck, Jake might, too. ATV is probably your best bet."

"Well, I'm done here," Westin announced, brushing his hands off. "Shall we check on that critter problem?"

"That's all you, buster," Kellie told him with a hard look. "Mystery critters are not my thing."

She waved them on toward the house, and Ford hopped the fence to walk with her, Westin jogging up behind them shortly. "I should be out of my session when they get here," Kellie told them both. "It's just a check-in with Gabby; she had a rough day yesterday. But if she needs to talk more, I can't promise it won't go late."

"Don't worry about it, Kells," Westin said easily. "It'll be fine."

"Which rooms are you putting the new arrivals in?" Ford asked as they walked toward the homestead house. "I'll plan on you not being there, just in case."

"Three, seven, and eight," Kellie recited as she tucked a strand of her blonde hair behind her ear. "You shouldn't have many of the other guests around, since they're doing their assigned chores, but make yourself at home while you wait."

Ford wasn't really interested in hanging out inside the house with nothing to do, just waiting for the new guests at the ranch to arrive as though he were some overeager employee. "Where are the dogs?" he asked instead. "I'll give them a good run or something, I'm sure they're feeling lazy."

"Oh, I don't even know," Kellie groaned with a wave of her hand. "They might be with Ryan. Just whistle. You know Casper and Frankie—if they're anywhere around, they'll come."

As suggested, Ford whistled his usual loud, piercing whistle he saved for calling the cows at home.

Distant barking answered him, and he laughed at the cheerful sounds of it before whistling again a few times, varying the tone of each in a singsong way.

"Ford, stop it!" Kellie laughed. "They'll be ridiculous—oh great, there they are. I'm going in. West, you know the way up to the attic?"

"Yeah, I got it," Westin replied as he jogged up the few steps to the porch of the house. "I'm gonna go up on the roof first anyway."

Kellie went into the house, and Westin disappeared around the corner of the porch to get to work.

The sound of panting came before the pounding paws crunched against the dried grass, and the gray-and-black freckled dogs bounded over to Ford as though he held a T-bone steak in each hand.

"Hey, boys," Ford greeted, crouching down and opening his arms to them. "Remember me?"

Frankie got to him first, going straight for the ear-scratching he expected Ford to give, while Casper circled them and continued to bark like he'd caught them both in some trap.

Casper had always been the less intelligent of the two.

"What are you lookin' at?" Ford asked Frankie in a playful tone. "Huh? What are you looking at?" He scratched and rubbed the dog, who flopped down on the ground and rolled to his back, his left hind leg kicking in time with Ford's scratching.

"Oh, you like that, huh? You like that, do you, boy?"

Casper, finally catching on, nudged his nose under Ford's arm, then up into his face, demanding attention for himself.

Ford leaned away a little, giving the dog a look. "And now you're interested, huh? Now you want some attention. Lucky for you, I've got two hands." He changed position and scratched both dogs for a minute, Casper choosing to sit close and encourage him rather than make a demonstration of himself.

"Sherlock's gonna hate the smell of you two on me," Ford grumbled with a reluctant smile. "He's a big guy, and he's not quite used to the heat yet, so he's napping at the cabin. Maybe we'll let you three roam around in a pasture together, huh? Make friends? What do you say?"

Neither dog seemed to take any interest in what he was saying, which Ford took to be a sign of agreement.

"How about some exercise, huh? I bet there are some tennis balls to toss your way somewhere . . ."

The dogs clearly knew the key word in that sentence, and immediately took off toward the back of the house.

"Well, okay, then," Ford said, getting to his feet and brushing bits of hair from his jeans before following them. The worn and stained tennis balls sat in a bucket on the back porch, and the dogs turned out to be possibly the best catchers he'd ever seen in dogs or humans. Everything he tossed, they snagged, and if they let it bounce, it only ever bounced once.

As much as he loved Sherlock, the only thing that dog ever did fast was eat.

That might have been partially his fault. When they were home in Montana, Sherlock loped in the pastures and chased whatever critters were too fast for him. Even in winter, the dog was trying to blend in with the cattle, moving when they moved and munching on hay with them.

If Ford had tried tossing a tennis ball at Sherlock, the dog would have sniffed it, then scooped it up in his mouth and wandered away without any interest in any sort of game or competition.

He was kind of like Ford in that sense. Maybe that was why they were so well-suited for each other.

A whistle turned Ford toward the house, and he saw Westin leaning out of an upper window. "Car approaching, Ford. Hop to it. Don't expect a tip."

"Find the critter yet?" Ford shouted up in return, waving him off.

Westin grinned and ducked back inside, giving nothing resembling an answer.

Ford sighed and tossed the tennis balls back out to the dogs before turning to head back around to the front of the house, wiping his hands off on his jeans, given the dirt and slobber that had gathered on his hands while he played with the dogs. Whoever the new guests were, there was no telling ahead of time if they had opinions about dirt and ranch life. Ford hadn't met all of the recent guests when he'd been around, only the ones who had felt particularly social or comfortable dining with a bunch of cowboys. Not all of them did, so he and the other guys had learned to be flexible with their plans outside of rodeo.

Just last month, dinner plans at the homestead had to be cancelled when one of the guests had a setback in her therapy when something in her situation triggered her. Kellie had been quick to send the message around that they couldn't do dinner, and it would be best if none of the guys, including Ryan, came around the homestead house for a couple of days. Considering the ranch was a place of healing and recovery for her guests, there was no problem in giving priority to them in things like this.

Dinner was easy enough to reconfigure, and a bunch of rodeo cowboys didn't need much to get by.

Ford paused at the corner of the house, leaning casually against the post of the porch as a dark blue sedan pulled up on the gravel. The driver lifted his fingers from the steering wheel in a classic Texas wave, and Ford responded by dipping the front of his hat.

He stepped forward as the car stopped, putting on his warmest smile. "Welcome to Broken Hearts Ranch," he greeted when the doors opened.

The tall woman in the front seat with short, dark hair smiled as she got out. "Welcoming committee?"

He shrugged. "More like a friendly neighbor doing a favor. Kellie's inside with another guest and asked me to help get y'all settled."

The woman made some noncommittal sound of acknowledgement. "Go figure. He says 'y'all' like a real cowboy. My name's Trish, cowboy. Yours?"

"Ford Hopkins, ma'am." He dipped the front of his hat, and glanced at the other two ladies exiting the car.

These two were tiny compared to Trish. The one nearest him was petite in every respect, almost unhealthily so, and everything about her seemed faded. She looked at Ford with wide eyes, and he knew instinctively that she would not want him any closer.

He only nodded at her, keeping his smile as gentle as he could.

"Josie," Trish said with surprising tenderness. "Come here, pumpkin. It's okay, he's gonna help with the bags."

Josie swallowed and scurried to her new friend's side, avoiding looking at Ford at all.

Poor thing, it was all he could do not to crouch down before her like she was a child and try to make her comfortable. But Kellie had talked to the Six about this enough that he knew there wasn't much he could do to help them. These guests needed to take their own action, and they needed the chance to call the shots in their life, since some of them had never had that kind of control.

Ford caught the eye of the driver and moved around to the back of the car to help with the bags, then stopped. The third woman stood there, clearly waiting for the same thing.

She wasn't as small as Josie, but he wouldn't put her much above five-foot-six. Her hair was long, wavy, and the color of honey, almost baffling in its perfect match, which made him want to run into Kellie's kitchen to find some. She wore skinny jeans, which had never fit any woman better, and her feet were encased in some strappy tan sandals his sisters would have fought over.

Not exactly ranch-approved footwear, but something about her red-painted toes made him want to smile.

"Don't worry about it, ma'am," Ford told her, thumbing his hat back just a little. "I'll get these."

Her bright green eyes snapped to his incredibly fast. "I can do it."

Ford frowned a little. "I mean no offense, ma'am . . ."

"Then don't say anything." Her right leg began to bounce a little while the driver popped the trunk.

"But Kellie asked me to handle the bags, and I don't think

she meant that anybody else couldn't," Ford went on politely, reaching in for the first suitcase. "It's just hospitality."

She sniffed and pulled the middle suitcase out of the trunk without any difficulty. "Doesn't matter. I'll do it myself."

Ford exchanged glances with the driver, whose pointedly widened eyes and shaking of his head told Ford that the drive from the airport had been interesting, if not entertaining. "Well, then I'll let you explain to Kellie why you're haulin' your own bags into her house when she specifically asked me to do it. Her house, her rules, and I'm thinking you don't want to start off on the wrong foot."

Her mouth tightened into a thin line, and her hold on the suitcase handle did as well. "I don't need your help."

"I'm not helping you," he shot back without malice. "I'm helping Kellie. So do me a favor and let go of your bag so I can get out of your way."

"Brynn," Trish all but barked. "For Pete's sake, let the Boy Scout get the bags, okay? Let's find our rooms!"

Brynn's mouth quirked in an almost smile that fascinated Ford. So she wasn't mad at everyone—just him. For no reason.

Interesting.

"Boy Scout," she murmured, nodding as she gave him a cursory look. "Yeah, that fits. Fine, take the bag, and get your merit badge." She released it and marched past him toward the others.

Ford exhaled in a rush, shaking his head at the driver. "Wow."

"Tell me about it," the driver muttered as he closed the trunk, the other suitcase in hand. "Where are we headed?"

CHAPTER 6

THERE WAS SOMETHING ABOUT this place that Brynn instantly liked. It had enough of the family farm feeling without sending her looking for an outhouse, and was cozy without being suffocating.

It was the opposite of suffocating, actually. There was space like she had never seen, and standing out on the porch looking out at the land was humbling and refreshing all at once.

A weight had lifted from her shoulders and chest from almost the moment they'd pulled in. Almost, because she had barked at the Boy Scout cowboy yesterday just for helping with the bags.

She'd apologized to Trish and Josie once they'd been alone, giving them a watered down explanation of her surges and how stresses like traveling could trigger her into irritability. Neither of them minded, but she had guilt about Boy Scout. He seemed like a good sort of guy; it wasn't his fault she only trusted about three men in the world now.

She did wonder how many girlfriends he had cheated on, but she tended to wonder that with every guy now.

Hazards of her past.

"Brynn?" Kellie's voice called.

"Yeah?"

Kellie herself appeared then, standing in the doorway behind the screen and smiling like an old friend. She'd only known the woman for fifteen hours, if that, but she was already one of Brynn's favorite people. She knew that would probably change when her therapy started in earnest. Yesterday, she had done her intake interview, and that had been relatively painless.

Relatively.

Kellie had asked her to start working on her walls, and her first assignment had been to write in her new Broken Hearts journal about what she wanted to get out of her time here, as well as identifying what her walls were.

The bigger question might have been what her walls were not.

Brynn was a fortress. Complete with dragons, a moat, an armed guard, and a firing squad.

She'd told Kellie as much, and Kellie had only smiled before telling her looking at the whole thing like that would make it harder to break each wall down.

The journal now had six dedicated pages on that idea.

"You okay?" Kellie asked, bringing Brynn back to the present.

"Yep, fine." Brynn nodded and smiled widely.

Kellie's eyes narrowed. "Rule of the ranch. 'Fine' is not an answer I accept. 'Fine' is a cop out. We're so used to saying it to not admit our thoughts and feelings and want everyone to assume we're always okay. It is okay to not be okay, all right? Especially here."

That was new information, and it took Brynn a moment to let it sink in. Somehow, Kellie's words seemed more like a life lesson than they might have been intended.

It is okay to not be okay.

When was the last time she'd actually been okay? Not moments of okay, but deeply okay.

"I'm nervous," Brynn admitted, her smile turning more hesitant. "I haven't opened up in a long time, and I'm afraid to hope something will help."

Kellie pushed open the screen and reached out a hand. "Now that's an answer I'll take. Come on in, we're gonna start a group session and introductions of our new guests."

Brynn took her hand, her brow furrowing in confusion. "You're not going to reassure me?"

"Strange, right?" Kellie all but beamed as they headed back into the house. "I've learned that I can tell people whatever comforting things I want, but until they are ready to face those fears, and step forward in spite of them, it won't do a darn thing. What you've just told me is normal, and sounds promising. More than that, you're gonna have to answer for yourself." She raised a brow and released her hand as she moved toward one of the chairs in the room where the other ladies were waiting.

Wow. Just . . . wow. The website for Broken Hearts had mentioned the working ranch aspect, but it seemed the therapy part of the place was just as much work, and maybe just as tough. Brynn hadn't dealt with therapists on a personal level, only a professional one for her patients, but she had a feeling Kellie Prosper was as rare as her ranch. And that seemed like reason enough to hope.

"Alrighty, gang," Kellie said to the room, "let's get started."

Brynn hurried to a kitchen chair that had been brought into the large great room for this group session and tucked some hair behind her ear. It had been a cool morning, so she had left her hair down, but one look around the room at the four other ladies who had been at the ranch already showed they all wore their hair up.

Then again, they'd been doing chores. Brynn probably wouldn't start those for a few more days, unless she really needed to work out some aggression, but she hadn't even looked at the list of chore options yet. She might not have the skills to do what would feel best.

Who trained the guests to do the chores? The image of that Boy Scout cowboy popped into her mind, and she frowned, wondering if he really was that good-looking, or if her memory was playing tricks.

Her memory did that from time to time.

"Hi, I'm Trish," Brynn's fellow newcomer announced from the couch, and she tuned in, apparently having missed the beginning of this thing. "I'm from Boston, but originally Pennsylvania, which is why you don't hear a Boston accent. I'm here because my twin sister died six months ago."

A sympathetic murmur resounded from the others, and Josie, who sat beside Trish, took her hand.

"Brain tumor," Trish went on, her voice wavering, her strong façade weakening. "And I've always felt she was the better twin. Married a great guy, had three terrific kids, genuinely liked people, could have been a fairytale princess that animals talked to . . . But I'm here and she's not. And I hate that."

It was impossible to not be moved by hearing that. Would they all have stories that made Brynn feel as though holes had been drilled through her heart?

The place was called Broken Hearts Ranch, so the answer might have been obvious, but she hadn't expected to feel the broken hearts around her in such a way.

Attention turned to Josie, who looked more like Trish's child than her fellow guest. Her eyes were almost colorless in their pale shade, and the wider they got, the more color they lost.

Trish put her arm around her and whispered something.

Josie swallowed and cleared her throat. "I'm Josie. From upstate New York. I . . . was in an abusive relationship for ten years. I finally got brave enough to leave and not go back."

"Good for you, sweet pea," a blonde with a thick twang in her voice praised, smiling at Josie with tenderness. "Hurts like a birch tree, don't it?"

The replacement phrase made Brynn smile even as Josie nodded fervently. "I haven't been able to restart my life since the divorce came through and I moved back in with my parents. I . . . don't know how."

Trish tightened her hold on Josie, rubbing her arm. "You'll find your voice, Josie. You will."

The others agreed with that, and Brynn nodded as well, though she suddenly wondered if her situation was pitiful compared to the others in this group. Death and abuse were huge things—practically insurmountable.

What did that make the cause of her broken heart?

Josie and Trish looked at her, followed by Kellie and the rest of the group.

Brynn had presented at several conferences professionally, had given reports to other physicians in grand rounds, and guest lectured at medical schools all over the Southwest without so much as batting an eyelash. But the prospect of talking about herself, about what had broken her, in front of seven other women started a cold sweat at the back of her neck.

"My name is Brynn," she began, her hands starting to shake in her lap. "I'm a doctor, recently divorced." Her throat suddenly went dry, and she struggled to swallow. "My ex is a pilot, and he . . . really enjoyed membership in the mile high club."

Someone in the room hissed in apparent pain, but a few others merely looked confused. The reference must have been lost on them.

She wet her lips, shifting in her chair. "And finding local tour guides with great legs."

Understanding seemed to dawn on the rest of them, and several heads were shaking in either disgust or sympathy.

"And drinks with coworkers that led to hotel rooms," Brynn went on, trying for a bitter smile, but finding her eyes burning with surprise tears. "But not starting a family with me."

Her voice caught on the last word, and she swallowed the growing lump. She couldn't cry over Minimus. Not now, not again, and not ever.

"And I'm angry about it," Brynn told them, finding her voice again. "Like, uncontrollably angry at times. Scary angry. If I ever snap at any of you, please know it isn't personal and I will feel sick with guilt as soon as I'm down from the surge. So I need help to be less angry. Or to be able to control it. One or the other, I guess. Preferably both."

"Why not both?" the blonde suggested, smiling brightly. "Let's do both!"

Brynn smiled back. "Sounds like a plan." She looked across the group at Kellie, only to find her smiling at her like a proud sister. But there was something else in her expression.

Understanding.

A deep, personal understanding that could only be explained by experiencing something similar.

Why that comforted Brynn, she couldn't quite say. She wouldn't want any woman to have experienced the things she had with Minimus—the shame and the embarrassment, the hurt and the insecurity—but knowing someone else would completely get where she was coming from and how she felt . . .

Full Rigged

That was something special.

Kellie knew her situation before Brynn arrived, but she hadn't seen this degree of understanding in their intake interview the day before. Why had it shown itself now? Or was Brynn only now seeing it?

Either way, she was suddenly even more delighted to be at this ranch, away from the noise of her life and among other women who were not expected to be perfect or normal all the time. Here, she could heal, because everyone else was healing, too.

She listened as the others introduced themselves quickly, the drill clearly familiar to them now. Sadie was the quirky blonde, halfway through her time at the ranch to heal after getting a diagnosis of infertility. Julia had brown hair that turned purple halfway through, and she was struggling to cope with the death of her mother. Paige was the picture of the farm girl next door, down to her dirty-blonde hair, freckles, and overalls, and her fiancé had left her the moment she'd received a cancer diagnosis. And Meredith, the most adorable auburn-haired woman Brynn had ever seen, was in her fifties and felt she had lost her identity when the last of her children had left home for college.

Had she looked at a report of the problems of the women here, of their situations and circumstances in life, there really was not much that was similar between them. Different wounds, different lives at home, different reasons for being here—simply different in every possible way. Yet there was a bond between the group now, a sisterhood of sorts that was difficult to explain, much less fully comprehend.

The only similarity was that they were all wounded and wanting to heal. Apparently, that was enough for these ties to form, and for a sense of unity to grow within Brynn.

She might be alone on this road, but she was not alone in the journey.

That could make all the difference.

"One of the things I want us to think about today is our emotions," Kellie told them all. "Each of you is at a different point in your journal assignments, but this will apply to everyone. Your experiences have created hurt, and anger, and depression, and so many other negative feelings. We have somehow expected ourselves to only feel happy things, so we fight against the bad ones. We refuse to accept them because we should be superhumans who never feel bad things. But we are not superhumans, and the sooner we accept that for ourselves, the better."

The women around the room all nodded, and Brynn, for one, immediately felt the truth of it. Her surges had been the worst when she had struggled against them and feared them. When she had tried to shove all of the anger and stress into some box or a corner. When the mere inkling of strong emotions of any kind, apart from happiness, rose up within her, she panicked.

All panic. All fear. All shame. All desperation to find a hole to hide herself in.

Because she was broken, and no one else could see.

Kellie seemed to be speaking directly to Brynn now, though her eyes met those of every woman there. "Acknowledge your emotions. All of them. Even the ugly and scary ones. Resisting them only lets them build up and makes them harder to deal with. Don't be ashamed of your strong emotions. Give them a voice. If it's not safe to express to people, write them out. Vent them on the page. If you don't have time to express them, take a minute to admit them to yourself. And when you have the time, give them that voice and that time. You owe it to yourself to have every emotion you feel."

Brynn glanced over at Trish and Josie, seeing them having a quiet conversation, and then Trish raised her hand.

"How should we fight the shame of our emotions?" she asked, the question clearly coming from Josie, but Trish's expression showed some concern herself. "Not fight, I guess, but . . . deal with it."

"Acknowledge it," Kellie said again with an approving nod. "There is nothing wrong with feeling."

Meredith was nodding, too. "What helps me is to take a few moments each day and pause to admit every feeling I have. I was used to just getting through each day without feeling anything, so I had to create a habit of admitting them even when I'm not feeling much at all. I'm not perfect at it, not by a long shot, but now it's easier, and the shame is lessening."

There was some comfort in that. If Meredith, if Paige, if any of the others who were here now and who had been here in the past could get their confusing, shameful, hurting emotions under control, regardless of the situation that had caused them, then maybe Brynn could do the same. Maybe she could manage her anger like any normal human being. Maybe she could admit the depth of her hurt, not only her anger.

Maybe she would feel less crazy and more like herself.

Broken Hearts Ranch could possibly heal more than her heart, if she would let it. She hadn't expected as much when Mandi had brought the idea to her. She'd simply been looking at it as an opportunity to get away from anything of her normal life or anything that would remind her of Minimus. Mandi had hit home on the idea of therapy while she got away, and Brynn could easily accept that she needed some sort of professional help, but if she simply had to wait until she returned to Albuquerque to seek out that part of it, so be it.

But here . . .

Here, she could get away from her normal life and her concerns, and get some professional help at the same time.

And she could do more than just sit around and contemplate her life. She could get out onto the land of the ranch and do physical work. Put her hands and arms and legs to work, and hopefully keep her mind from obsessing on things of the past.

Reflection would come when Kellie asked her to, and when she was doing the exercises and assignments as instructed. But she would not let herself get overly focused on every emotion of every day. The point was to keep living, and to learn how to live with those emotions as they rose and fell.

She would find a way. Here in this place, she could find it.

Chapter 7

"I don't understand how any of you enjoy this place. I mean really, this is awful."

Ford all but rolled his eyes as Lars complained yet again while they all worked on a fence in one of the west pastures.

"I never hear Ford crying about the heat," Ryan pointed out, wiping at his sweat-dampened brow with the sleeve of his T-shirt.

Lars straightened from his position with the post-hole digger. "Ford hates the heat, too, don't you?"

Eric, Ryan, and Westin all looked at Ford then, just as Lars was, and he returned their looks without concern, shrugging a little. "Does anybody like heat?"

"That's not an answer!" Eric protested as he wiped his work gloves off on each other.

"Come on, man!" Lars cried. "Montana boys gotta stick together!"

Ford leaned on the portion of fence they'd already finished, this conversation getting old for how often they had it. "Yeah, it's hot. Not my favorite. But I don't really care."

Lars frowned at his answer. "Don't really care about being baked in this oven of Mother Nature? Really?"

There really wasn't anything to do but shrug again. "Just because you think this is the devil's armpit doesn't mean I have to."

"I believe that is three points for Texas," Ryan announced with a laugh. "Come on, last section, and then we can head back. Kells says we're invited to dinner at the ranch."

Ford looked at him with mild interest. "Really? With the guests or without? I know she wasn't all that excited about us coming around last night with the new ones, and you know we don't want to intrude on that."

"According to her text, it's fine." Ryan made the facial equivalent of a shrug. "She's talked with them, and they all know they don't have to be there if they don't want to. None of them have anything against men in the house."

The image of the little timid one he'd met yesterday came to Ford's mind, and he shook his head. "Maybe check again. One of the ones I got the bags for yesterday was looking at me like I had horns and had crawled out from under her bed. There's no way she's okay with six cowboys coming into the house she's staying in, not unless Kellie's sessions are working a lot faster than any other times I've been around."

"Well, did you crawl out from under her bed?" Westin asked with a raised brow. "That could scare anyone."

Ford gave him a hard look. "How'd the critter catch go, West? Come out of it unscathed?"

Considering West currently had a pair of angry scratches on his left jawline, there was no argument against it. He scowled at Ford and carried the post they would be placing over to the hole Lars had just finished. "Let's get this done. At least three of us are going to need showers before Kellie lets us in the house."

They worked quickly and methodically, Ford pouring gravel into the hole, Eric working the tamper while Ryan and West handled the cement mixture. Ford and Lars maintained the post in its place while the others worked around it.

"You might want to use limestone," Lars suggested as he watched the process. "This kind of ground might take a limestone-concrete combination well."

Ford caught Ryan's short exhale and clamped down on his lips to keep from laughing. Darren made the same sound frequently when Ford overstepped, especially when he had another plan in mind.

"We're doing additional crushed gravel on top," Ryan told him. "That's why we haven't been filling the holes completely with cement, if you haven't noticed."

Lars lifted his fingers off the post, leaving his palms in place, a clear sign of surrender. "Fair enough. That was my next suggestion."

"Of course it was," Eric muttered with a sly smirk.

Ford snorted very softly. "Right, so when do you want to do the rest of the gravel? Tonight?"

Both Ryan and Lars shook their heads, but Ford did Ryan the respect of only looking at him in anticipation of the answer. "We'll let it settle overnight. It's fast-set concrete, but if we put the gravel in now, we'd still have to come back and do more. The gravel on the bottom has been tamped, but we'll wait for the concrete to set and settle before coming back." Ryan set the bucket down and put his hands on his hips, eying this final hole.

"Where's Caleb when you need him?" Westin grunted grumpily. "He should be out here doing this with us."

Ryan laughed once. "There's more than one job to be done around here. Caleb's teaching the more experienced guests how to herd the cattle. I'm sure it'll be entertaining."

"The last time you said that," Eric laughed, "Lindsey was the one laughing at Caleb."

"I miss Lindsey," Westin said with a playfully sad sigh. "She could outwork Reid like nobody's business."

Ford tsked loudly at the jab. "Cheap shot to attack the man when he isn't here to hear or defend it."

"It's good practice," West replied without concern. "Gotta make sure I can get him good when he gets back from D.C."

"I'll make sure Kells puts a note from you both in the follow-up call to Lindsey now that she's back home," Ryan told them both dryly. "I think we're done for now. It's set enough. Pile in the truck, let's go."

"Yes, sir," at least three of them said at the same time, which led to a round of snickering as they headed to Ryan's truck with the equipment.

Ford hopped into the bed of the truck and took the tamper from Eric, setting it down carefully. Eric moved up to the passenger seat of the truck while Lars and Westin joined him in the bed with the buckets, post digger, and cement bags. They settled in, and Ford tapped the top of the truck's cabin to signal Ryan when they were set.

The drive back to Ryan's cabin was dusty and bumpy, as one might expect for a Texas ranch road, but the dry breeze was welcome. Not exactly cooling, but nice all the same.

They stopped at the barn to drop off the equipment, then headed to the cabins to clean up and change. Ford and Eric moved to theirs, and Sherlock was quick to greet them at the door without any barking or fanfare, though he did sniff them eagerly.

"How many times do I have to tell you to leave the bulls outside?" Eric teased with a grin, scratching Sherlock's ears.

"I know, right?" Ford snorted softly and patted the dog's back. "Monster."

"I'll get him fed if you want to jump in the shower," Eric offered. "I need to check the channel anyway."

Ford rolled his eyes and laughed. "Oh, yeah, Rodeo King. Gotta keep the fame up. You gonna livestream dinner tonight?"

Eric scowled at him. "One more comment like that, and I'll livestream your shower."

Generally speaking, that was beyond Eric's nature, but he was also really good at surprising people, so who was to say he would not sneak into the bathroom and film him mid-shower?

Suddenly, the idea wasn't all that funny.

"Right," Ford said slowly, "I'll just be five minutes." He left without waiting for a reply, and was quick to clean himself of the dirt and sweat of the day. Kellie was a ranch girl, so she might not necessarily expect them to clean up after a day of work, but there were the other guests staying there who might not be as familiar with the ways of a working ranch. And Ford didn't mind showing respect to Kells, or them, by taking a few minutes to look and smell like he hadn't rolled around in dirt and grass all day.

Once he'd put on a clean pair of jeans and a shirt, and Eric had done the same, they headed next door with Sherlock in tow, met up with the others, and all started the walk to the homestead house.

It was a trip Ford had taken dozens of times over the years, and every time, he'd wondered if they were almost there just before they arrived. It was no different tonight, and his stomach was growling eagerly as they stepped up onto the porch.

"Come on in!" Kellie called as they appeared at the screen door of the kitchen. "And someone set the table!"

"Got it!" Eric replied, no doubt to give himself something

easy to do instead of whatever else Kellie might need help with.

The rest of them rolled their eyes and removed their hats as they entered, as Kellie usually requested.

"What else needs doing?" Ryan asked his sister, patting down his slightly messy hair.

Kellie paused whatever she was stirring and pointed. "Bread on the table, butter, honey, jam, all the accessories. Potatoes and carrots, salad, get the dressings. Whichever one of you can do it best, come over here and shred the pot roast. Sessions went on too long, so I don't have my guests in here helping right now. A handful are joining us, so Eric, make sure you set all the plates I put out!"

Eric saluted, though she wouldn't see it.

"Hey, Kells," Ryan said, coming over to the pot roast and putting a hand on her back. "Breathe. Just us. Not an emergency."

"I know," she grunted. "Just rushed."

Ford shared a look with West and Lars, and the three of them moved into the kitchen to silently pick up the other things and take them to the table, arranging them neatly among the settings Eric was laying out.

"Drinks," West said, looking around at stuff. "Water? Soda?"

"There's raspberry lemonade, too!" Kellie announced without looking up. "Paige whipped it up today."

"I'll have that," Ford ordered, raising a finger at West.

"Make it two," Eric chimed.

"Water here," Lars said as he carried the butter, jam, and honey to the table.

"We'll all have lemonade," a woman announced as she and two others entered the room, one of whom had purple in her hair that caught Ford by surprise. Then he saw the woman with honey-colored hair who'd given him a hard time the other day with the bags.

Brynn, he reminded himself.

She didn't look much happier today, which made him wonder if she ever was.

Kellie grinned at the guests, seeming relieved to see them. "Hi, ladies. We're almost ready. Take whatever seats you want." She frowned a little. "I knew Josie wanted to stay back, but what about Trish?"

"She's staying with Josie for support," the purple-haired lady said. "And Meredith and Sadie are hitting up Lost Creek tonight, so Paige, Brynn, and I are it."

"I thought they might." Kellie grinned and gestured to the room. "These are the guys. Some of them should look familiar, but I'm not sure you guys will know Ford. He's not been back long. And Brynn's new, so you won't know any of them except maybe my brother Ryan." She jabbed his shoulder pointedly, which Ryan reacted dramatically to.

"I know West and Lars," Purple Hair said, pointing to each. "We met when I was making a fool of myself with the cows last week."

Lars chuckled. "It wasn't that bad, Julia. Nice to see you again." He indicated Eric and Ford for them all. "Eric is the scrawny one, and Ford is the less scrawny one."

"Hey," Purple Hair and a blonde woman said, both waving easily. Brynn said nothing, though her eyes did widen as she saw Ford.

It was all he could do not to say something, but he only smiled and nodded to them as a collective.

Brynn looked over at Kellie. "Is there anything we can help with, Kellie? Or Ryan, was it?"

The siblings exchanged looks, then looked at each other's food item, nodding in almost eerie synchrony. "I think we're ready, actually. Just have a seat. Thanks, Brynn."

They all moved to the table and sat, before Kellie smiled down the table. "Eric, would you say grace for us?"

Brynn looked surprised and glanced at her fellow guests, both of whom were clearly used to this and had already bowed their heads.

"Lord, we thank you for the day that we've had and the work our hands and hearts have been able to do,' Eric began. "We thank you for this ranch and for Kellie's vision for it. We're grateful for the food on this table and the hands that prepared it, and ask that it nourish and strengthen us. Help us to improve ourselves each day and help the guests here to heal in whatever ways they need. In Jesus' name we pray, amen."

"Amen," the table answered.

"Thanks, Eric," Kellie said with a smile. "All right, dig in!"

There was some shuffling as bowls of food and utensils moved around the table, but it wasn't long before they were all chatting easily and eating.

"Need a lifeguard for your pot roast there, West?" Ford asked around a bite of potatoes. "It's drowning."

West looked down at his gravy-drenched pot roast before glancing at Ford in derision. "Mind your own business."

Ford shrugged as Ryan snorted a laugh. 'Can do. Just thought Kells might want to know why there's no gravy left but plenty of pot roast. Dry leftovers it is."

"I can make more gravy," Kellie laughed, dabbing at her mouth with a napkin.

"Nope, no extra work for you," Lars announced with a firm shake of his head. "That's not allowed. We'll just shame West until he apologizes."

West mopped up some gravy with a slice of buttered bread and took a bite, shrugging without any sort of apology.

"Are they always like this?" Ford heard Brynn ask Kellie.

"Always," Kellie told her. She winked, then looked at the rest. "Someone explain to Brynn here who y'all are."

Ryan laughed at that and smiled at the guest. "So we all went to the same community college back in the day. Sam Houston Community College, which is pretty much on the other side of Lost Creek and then like half an hour. We decided to start up a rodeo team, and we were pretty good, so we were dubbed the Original Six."

"By whom?" Brynn asked, apparently not entirely impressed. "Yourselves?" At least three people coughed a laugh, which made Brynn wince before looking at Kellie. "Sorry..."

"It's fine," Kellie told her, rubbing her arm. "These guys don't take offense easily. Do you want to introduce yourself or do you want me to?"

Brynn shook her head. "I'll do it." She exhaled shortly and managed a small smile, which caught Ford somewhere under his sixth rib. "My name's Brynn Kershaw. I'm a doctor in Albuquerque. I'm here because—"

"We don't need to know," Ryan said quickly, cutting her off with a smile. "It can stay private; we don't need to know anything you don't feel like sharing. We're used to it."

"I am here," Brynn said a little louder, grounding it out, "because I've been angry since the day I found out my husband has never been faithful to me in any relationship we've ever had. And I lash out. Everything irritates me. So, for example, right now I want to toss the rest of the bread at Ryan's face for interrupting me, even though I know he was trying to be kind and considerate and had absolutely no intention of making me upset in any way. And that is my issue, not his, so I'm sorry, Ryan, that I want to throw bread at your face. Kellie wants me to identify my feelings, and that's my feeling right now."

The table was silent for a moment, and then Paige laughed, clapping her hands once. "Oh lands, Brynn, I know you said you've gotten more honest since then, too, but good night, that could have stayed to yourself!"

The tension broke, and an uneasy laughter started from a few of them, Brynn included.

"Maybe I'll catch the bread in my mouth," Ryan suggested, smiling in his easy way. "Sorry for cutting you off."

"I didn't think about filters," she admitted, groaning even as she smiled, and put her face in her hands.

Kellie rubbed her back soothingly. "If you're gonna be blunt, this is the group for that. You already know Julia and Paige are easy enough to be around, and I think these guys could be roped in there."

"I doubt it," Brynn said, raising her head with a heavy exhale. "I'm always worse with men. Nothing but honesty flies with me anymore. And I always ask really awful questions to test their honesty. I've been on three dates since the divorce, and none of them lasted more than fifteen minutes."

"You're just dating the weak," West boasted with a laugh. "And that's not a pickup line, I'm happily and honestly in a relationship."

Brynn's green eyes darted to him. "Think you can take it?"

"Why not?" Westin shrugged with utensils in hand and continued to eat. "I don't ruffle easily, nothing to hide."

Julia shook her head. "Uh-oh."

Brynn narrowed her eyes, her lips twisting a little. "What is your least favorite part of Ryan's personality?"

Lars thumped the table as he laughed, and Eric grinned like it was Christmas. Westin, however, looked as though he'd bitten the inside of his cheek in an attempt to chew his potato.

His hesitation made Brynn smirk. "Honesty too difficult?"

"Ryan isn't very decisive," West finally grumbled, his grip on his fork tightening. "Has to think longer than I'd like."

Brynn's smirk morphed to a smile, and she looked at Ryan for confirmation. "Well?"

Ryan made a face. "I'm thinking it over."

A snort of laughter escaped Brynn, which made Ford and the rest laugh.

Turning her attention to Lars, Brynn raised a brow. "Sorry, what was your name again?"

"Lars," came his reply as he straightened in his seat. "Fire away."

"Why did your last relationship fail?" she asked without missing a beat.

Poor Lars coughed in surprise, any hint of smugness gone. "Well . . . I guess I just didn't see her as wife material."

"And what constitutes wife material?" Brynn shot back.

Lars drummed his fingers on the table, his discomfort obvious. "Being able to run a ranch. She couldn't do that, so it wouldn't have worked."

"Was that why?" Eric mused, smiling a little.

He should have kept his mouth shut, since Brynn turned to him next. "Do these jeans make me look fat?" she asked, rising from her seat and stepping back for him to see.

Eric paled noticeably, but gave her an obedient look. "Uh . . . No. But they do enhance your hips with your shirt tucked in like that."

Brynn snorted softly and nodded at him. "Good save." She looked at Ford then, her mouth forming a tight line.

He met her gaze easily, finding more fascination than fear in him at the moment.

"This is an easy one," Ryan said with a wave of his hand. "Ford's as honest as they come—nothing gets to him."

"That right, Boy Scout?" Brynn asked, tilting her head to one side.

"Boy Scout?" Lars repeated. He turned in his chair, giving Ford a look. "How long's that been a name?"

Ford shrugged at them both, waiting for his question.

Brynn folded her arms, still standing. "Do you want kids?"

"Yep."

"How many?"

"Enough to run a ranch, not enough to make me crazy." He smiled at his own response. "Honest enough?"

Eric whistled low. "Not even a flinch. Can we do this every time? Ford should be named Cool Hand Luke. Go again, Brynn. Ask him another one."

Brynn ignored him and continued to stare at Ford, despite the fact that he'd answered her question with complete honesty. "Have you ever been unfaithful to a woman?"

"No," Ford said with a firm shake of his head.

"Got any proof?"

He smiled a little, amused that she asked for proof from him when there had been no such requests for anyone else. "Two sisters who can grill me better than anyone I've ever met, and analyzed every relationship I've had since I was seventeen. Want their numbers?"

Westin started snickering as he continued to eat like the bottomless pit he was.

"Can I look through your texts?" Brynn asked next.

Ford reached into his back pocket and pulled out his phone, setting it on the table. "Sure. Pass code is 695847."

Brynn looked at the phone, then at Eric, who sat closest to it. "Would you check that, please, Eric?"

"And it's not even my birthday," Eric said gleefully, plucking the phone from the table and entering the code for all to see.

When the phone unlocked, the table cheered like they were at a bar and someone had downed an epic shot.

Full Rigged

Ford only smiled, wondering if she would ask him something else.

Brynn seemed to be suppressing a smile herself, though he could tell that none of the fight had gone out of her. A few wavy strands of her hair fell across her brow, but she didn't seem to notice. "Are you for real, Boy Scout?"

The question had no edge to it, which was a first, and almost sounded like a private question just for him. Her voice had softened, her volume dropped, and a true note of curiosity accompanied it.

Strangely enough, all of that made it harder to answer.

"As far as I know," he told her, shrugging. "Never been very good at pretending."

Now Brynn did smile, and it was more captivating than a Texas sunrise.

And all he wanted to do was keep watching it.

"I'll vouch for that," Ryan groaned loudly. "Once, the rodeo was short a bullfighter, and Ford got pulled to help out. Those are the guys dressed up as clowns, right? And Ford was pitiful. Absolute disgrace of a showman and entertainer. You've never seen a more depressing clown in your life."

Ford only smirked at the story as the others joined in, every one of them getting their jabs in at his expense. He wouldn't rise to it or refute anything, especially since most of it was true, and because keeping this connection with Brynn suddenly seemed more important than anything he'd done in days.

He would not look away, not until she did, and maybe not even then. She continued to stare at him, her smile in place but shifting between degrees as she sat and pretended to join the conversation.

What had she seen in him, in his answers and honesty, that made her smile like that?

And how could he do it again?

CHAPTER 8

"You had to pick hay bales, didn't you, Brynn? Just had to decide that was the chore you wanted to start with," she huffed to herself as she hauled one of the bales from the pile in the barn and set it down in the bed of a truck, her fingers burning inside the work gloves as she released another line of twine. She'd only done six other bales, but she was already dying.

"Caleb!" she barked toward the other side of the stack, wiping her hand across her sopping brow. "There's gotta be an easier way to do this! Can't I just line up the truck with the bales and push them over?"

Caleb, her boss for the day, snorted a laugh from his side. "You can try, Doc, but how good is your aim? And remember, we can't break any of them."

She glared, even though he wouldn't be able to see it. "If I'd known I was going to be doing stuff like this, I'd have started a weight training program before I got here."

"What did you think they meant by ranch life and chores?" she heard Caleb ask, and wondered if he was still laughing at her. "Mowing the lawn?"

Brynn muttered under her breath, shaking her head and reaching for another bale of hay.

It had been like this all day, and though she was irritable with how her hands and arms and back ached, she could honestly say this was the most satisfying day she'd had on the ranch so far. She hadn't even been here a week, but the focus for the first few days had been settling in and taking stock of the more therapeutic needs she would have during her time here. It was interesting to see how structured the schedule and details were for the place in some respects, yet how adaptable and individualized they were, too. Josie, for example, was not doing chores yet, and had two sessions a day with Brynn besides the daily group session. Paige had two sessions a week and was almost constantly out on the ranch doing work.

Everyone else was somewhere in the middle, and no one's day looked the same.

If she had not seen it herself, Brynn would have sworn that an army of people handled the actual therapy side of things. But Kellie was a one-woman show, and the army of people working there was strictly on the ranch part of the equation.

That had to exhaust the woman, but she seemed to have an endless amount of energy without being the annoying, bubbly type of person.

Yet she wasn't invincible. Just that morning, Brynn had sat in the kitchen with her, both of them nursing mugs of coffee, and they'd quietly chatted while the others slept. Kellie had seemed tired in a way that going back to bed would not fix.

Tired, but not drained.

It shouldn't have made sense, but Brynn understood. She had weeks of feeling the same way in her medical practice, where the monotony of her day-to-day wore on her for one reason or another, yet she was still able to find motivation to keep going.

There was always something especially rewarding that came at the end of those times, something that renewed her passion for medicine and helped her find the energy she'd lacked.

But she didn't have a practice like Kellie did.

Would it make a difference if she did?

She hadn't loved working in medicine for a long time. Since the divorce, actually.

Scratch that. Since the truth had come out, which ultimately led to the divorce.

It had been a fantastic distraction from all of that mess, allowed Brynn to compartmentalize everything, and gave her something constructive to focus on while lawyers talked. While Minimus tried to charm her into settling, she was able to devote herself to patient care and her training. Yes, she had taken on some additional shifts working Urgent Care when possible to avoid her home while all of that went on, but all in all, her avoidance was still productive.

But all of that had since become just the drudgery of day in and day out work. Nothing to differentiate one day from the next, except for a special brand of stupidity that inevitably emerged from at least one patient each day.

Some of them still called her Dr. Gable by mistake, which felt like a slap in the face each time, given her emotional surges. Always an accident, and she'd smile and gently correct them, then move on.

In theory.

In reality, the anger clawed at her stomach until she could go to her office and react however she needed to, be it diving into her chocolate stash, digging her fingers and nails into a stress ball, or banging her head against the desk.

She needed something new and different, something she hadn't been dealing with or doing when she had been married to or dealing with Minimus. She'd rearranged her office at work as much as she could, she'd moved out of their house and into a gorgeous condo fit for a successful single woman, she'd gotten a full makeover, and she'd had her lawyer set up a "Do Not Contact" order against Minimus when it was clear he had no intention of severing ties despite ending their marriage. She'd traded in her car, taken back her maiden name, joined a gym, created online dating profiles, and taken a trip solo that did not involve education or networking.

Everything she had found as suggestions for coping with divorce, she had done.

Why didn't it feel like enough?

"Brynn? Brynn, are you in here?"

Brynn picked up another bale of hay, twisting to call over her shoulder, "Yeah!" She moved to the truck and dropped the bale in line with the others and set her gloves at her hips while she waited for whoever had called her.

Kellie appeared around the front of the truck, finding Brynn on the pile of bales immediately. "I'm so sorry to do this to you, but we need a doctor."

It took a moment for the words to really sink in, but then Brynn blinked and nodded. "Right, what's going on?" She hopped down from her position on the pile and tugged off her gloves, setting them aside. "You good, Caleb?"

"Yeah, Doc, see you later!" he called, still out of sight.

Brynn smiled as reassuringly at Kellie as she could without any context. "What can I do, Kellie?"

Kellie shook her head, sighing. "I just got a call from Jenny, Caleb's wife. She was helping with making the jam today. Julia passed out while they were working in there, and they've got her out of the kitchen now—said it was hot and humid, but no more than it has been any other time."

"Do you know if she was feeling okay this morning?" Brynn asked as they hurried out of the barn.

"I'm not sure," Kellie admitted, heading to an ATV still running nearby. "They were still trying to get her cooled down and lucid when I got the call. I just bolted from the office and grabbed the ATV. If we didn't have you on site, I'd have called Doc Mills in Lost Creek, which we've done before, and we still can, if you'd prefer..."

Brynn turned to her before getting on the ATV. "Kells, it's fine. I'm happy to help. Let's go, and I'll see what I can do."

It was a short drive to the homestead house, and both women were quick to climb off the ATV when they got there.

Brynn hustled into the house, moving to the kitchen first to wash her hands. "You okay, Jules?" she called, seeing a few women gathered around a figure on the couch.

"Maybe?" came a weak, laughing response. "I don't feel sick, just... off."

Drying her hands on a hand towel, then shaking them out as well, Brynn went to the couch.

Julia lay there with a damp rag across her brow, her feet propped up on throw pillows, looking pale but smiling. Her dark hair was pulled back, only little hints of the purple-dyed sections visible.

Trish and Josie got up from their places on the floor to give Brynn space, but they still hovered nearby in concern. Brynn pulled over an ottoman and sat on it, taking Julia's wrist gently in hand and feeling for her pulse. "What happened, sweetie?"

Julia exhaled slowly, closing her eyes. "We were making jam in the kitchen. I wasn't feeling great, little bit of a headache, but I figured I hadn't had enough water. I was watching my pot for the bubbles, and I started getting really hot. Started feeling fuzzy from the neck up, and also in my fingers. I'd been leaning against the counter, so I straightened up, and that was a bad idea. As soon as I straightened my legs, everything started to buzz harder. Vision started getting fuzzy, and then I was falling."

"I caught her," Trish broke in, putting a hand on Julia's elevated feet and smiling. "Josie and I brought her out here away from the heat of the kitchen. She was pretty clammy, and took a while to start making sense again."

"I thought it might be her blood sugar," Josie volunteered in an almost whimper. "I have a sister who's diabetic, so I got some juice for her, thinking it might help . . ."

Brynn smiled at the young woman, knowing what a big deal it was for her to say anything with confidence. "Great idea. That's one of my first go-to solutions, too."

Josie's smile could have lit the room, but it vanished quickly as her cheeks flamed in embarrassment.

Poor thing. Brynn should make more of an effort there. Josie could use as much encouragement as possible, and as many friends as she could get.

"Pulse seems fine," Brynn told Julia, turning her attention back. "Do you pass out frequently?"

"No, almost never." Julia smiled a little. "I haven't felt sick to my stomach, I'm not congested, I haven't been feeling particularly anxious . . ."

Brynn's eyes narrowed in thought. "Does your vision go spotty if you stand up too fast?"

"Only if I've been lying down for a while," Julia said with a slight shrug. "And it clears really fast."

"Any problems with blood pressure in your medical history?"

"No, it's always been pretty good."

Brynn nodded in thought, an idea prickling in the back of her mind that she didn't think she should say in front of the others. "Would you be okay if I take you into town? I just want to check a few things, but I'm not overly concerned. I just need a few of the things they'll have at the clinic."

Julia nodded, pulling the damp cloth from her head. "Yeah, sure." She sat up quickly, her eyes widening as she did so. "Whoa."

"Don't rush it," Brynn ordered quickly, grabbing her arm in case she passed out again. "Nice and easy. Josie, could you grab a bottle of water for her?"

"Yep." Josie bolted for the kitchen as though Julia's life depended on it.

Brynn glanced at Kellie, who was standing behind them. "Is there a car I can use, Kellie?"

"I don't have a ranch truck available right now," Kellie admitted with a frown. "Ryan's got them out in the fields. My personal truck's in the shop. Let me see what I can do." She pulled out her phone, her thumbs flying across the screen. "I'll text Dr. Mills, too, just so he knows you're coming."

"Thanks." Brynn pushed to her feet and gave Julia a steady look as Josie returned with a bottle of water. "How are you feeling now?"

She took the bottle from Josie with a smile. "The room isn't spinning, so that's good, right?"

Brynn nodded. "I'll take that. Can you drink that before we get to the clinic? Just in case dehydration is part of it. Don't chug, though."

"I'll do my best," Julia quipped. "Can I stand up?"

"Sure, if you feel like it." Brynn held out her hands, which Julia took, and slowly, she rose without wobbling. "Looking good. Let's get you some shoes."

"On it!" Trish called, dashing off to the bedrooms.

Julia looked after her in consternation. "I have shoes right here from when we were making jam. Honestly, what kind of shoes does she think I need?"

Brynn could only shake her head. "Hopefully something easy for Texas in June, right?"

"Totally."

"Okay, Ford's bringing his truck over. He'll drive you guys to the clinic," Kellie announced to them both.

"Boy Scout?" Brynn asked, a little startled. "Doesn't he have things to do?"

Kellie nodded as she tucked her phone away. "Yeah, he has to go into Lost Creek to test out a new hazer, so it's perfect."

Whatever a hazer was, Brynn didn't have a chance to ask, since Trish ran back into the room with a pair of Julia's sandals.

"That's what you had to get?" Julia asked with a laugh when Trish stooped down to help her with the shoes.

"Texas in summer, hon." Trish gave her a stern look. "Gotta show off those cute toes when you're not working on the ranch."

Julia seemed to consider that. "Well, I did get a pedicure before I got here, and it's still in good shape."

"Exactly." Trish gave her a wink, patting her ankle once the sandals were on.

Brynn took the chance to go to her room and grab her own phone, wondering how good Uber was in Lost Creek for when they needed to get back to the ranch after.

Unless Boy Scout wouldn't take that long . . .

She wasn't about to ask him, though. There was something about the guy that she liked, but there was also something that made her nervous. Most men didn't make her nervous anymore, probably because she saw them with the same brand of loathing as Minimus.

It hadn't always been that way, though. She'd adored him in the early days, been completely swept off her feet, and happy beyond any of her expectations. He'd been Prince

Charming, her personal comedian, and the only set of arms that could truly hold her at her most vulnerable.

She had a journal entry to write about him soon, and she was putting it off.

Dwelling on Minimus was heartbreaking and disgusting now, bringing hordes of regret and shards of guilt along with it.

She wouldn't have thought of him now, except that he had made her nervous at the very beginning. His ridiculous good looks and easy nature made his interest in someone like her seem too good to be true.

Ford making her nervous scared her, even if it was on a smaller scale. He was a good-looking guy, no question there, and the raw manliness of his cowboy stature and self-confidence screamed out to be appreciated, but that's not what made her nervous. Attractive guys were everywhere.

It was the way her stomach had flipped when he'd smiled at her the other night. She hadn't felt anything for a guy except animosity in ages, and feeling that . . .

That made her nervous.

Ford might be more honest than Minimus, was undoubtedly classier than Minimus, and could not have looked more different from her ex had he been a cat, but that didn't mean Brynn could trust him.

Not completely.

Not yet.

Maybe not ever.

That was her problem, when she thought about it.

Trust.

That deserved a journal entry, too.

When she was able.

Shaking her head, Brynn turned out of her room and went back to the front of the house, where the others were. "Okay, ready?"

Julia nodded, and Brynn put a hand at her back, offering support without making it look like the woman needed to actually be carried out of the house.

Ford's black truck sat in front of the house and he leaned against the passenger door, waiting for them. He tipped the front of his hat as they approached. "Ladies."

"I'm so sorry about this," Julia said weakly before Brynn could say anything. "I feel like an idiot."

"Why?" Ford asked with a tilt to his head as he opened the truck's door. "If the doc here thinks you need to get checked out, that's nothing to apologize for. I'm headed that way anyway, might as well drop you off." He held out a hand to help Julia up onto the runner and into the truck. Once she was settled, he closed the door and turned to the cabin's passenger side door. "Sorry, Doc, I wasn't sure if she was the carsick sort or not. My sister has to sit in the front when she gets like this. Do you mind sitting in the back?"

Brynn blinked at the thoughtfulness Ford had for Julia, and at being asked that question. "No, that's fine. I don't know if she gets carsick, actually. Probably a good idea."

Ford paused, smiling a little and making her stomach flop when he did so. "A huntin' dog couldn't find a compliment in there if he tried."

"Don't get your kerchief in a twist, Boy Scout," Brynn mumbled, a reluctant smile taking control of her mouth. "There's no merit badge for thinking."

"I'll give you that one." Ford grinned now, and it yanked on her stomach like a tug of war. He opened the door, offering the same hand to her he'd offered to Julia.

There was no telling what her stomach might do if she took that hand, and she didn't need the help anyway, so she stepped forward and reached for the grab handle herself, stepping onto the runner. "Got it, thanks."

Ford's hand dropped. "Least you said thanks this time.

Maybe I'm getting there." He clicked his tongue and walked around the truck to his side, still smiling.

That was not cute, and it was not funny.

So why did it make her want to giggle?

Closing the door and buckling in, she shook her head. "You okay, Jules?

"Yeah, I feel pretty good now. The AC in here is nice." Julia sighed in delight as she turned the vents more toward her. "If Texas had any cool breezes in June, that would have helped."

"Blast the air all you want," Ford told her as he got in. "I'm from Montana; the cold doesn't bother me."

Brynn unexpectedly snorted a laugh at the particular reference that phrase created in her mind. For all his efforts, there was no way Ford could relate to an animated ice queen, but the wording was a nice touch.

Ford met her eyes in the rearview mirror, somehow smiling in them. "Thanks, Doc. Can't unsee that, huh?"

She shook her head, biting down on her lips hard. She scooted forward, fighting the laughter rising within her. "Jules, I need to ask you a question. Boy Scout, shut your ears."

"Yes, ma'am." He immediately focused intently on the gravel road before them and began to hum.

"Julia," Brynn asked in a much softer voice, "is there any chance you could be pregnant?"

Julia whirled around in her seat and stared at Brynn with wide eyes. "What?"

Brynn covered Julia's hand on the seat. "I'm just saying, it's a possibility based on what you've told me. Is there a chance?"

"No . . . I mean, I guess . . ." Julia's brow creased and her eyes widened. "Oh my word, Brynn . . . Yeah. Yeah, I could be. I'm late. I thought it was the stress—it's been spotty since . . . But yeah, I really could be."

"Okay." Brynn nodded, rubbing Julia's hand soothingly. "Then you're going to want to finish that bottle of water before we get to the clinic. We'll want a sample to test."

Julia giggled a little right before her eyes began to well up. "Brynn . . . I want my mom for this. If this is happening, I'll want her so much. What do I do?"

It was as though Brynn's heart actually cracked in two. "Right now, you wait. And you hold my hand. And if this is happening, you're gonna call your husband. What's his name?"

"Alex."

"You're gonna call Alex," Brynn told her, "and you're gonna laugh or cry or both, and then we're gonna go back to the ranch and you'll talk to Kellie. We don't need to think beyond that, okay?"

Julia nodded and swallowed. "Okay." She exhaled roughly before smiling. "Thanks for not asking me that in front of the others. They'd all get excited and then disappointed if it didn't happen, and I don't want to hype things up if it's not happening. I'm not even texting Alex until we know."

"I get it." Brynn returned her smile. "And if it is happening, I won't say a word. You don't have to either. The other guests don't need to know. Kellie should, given she's in charge, and how this could impact your journey to recovery, but nobody else needs to know unless you really want to tell them. I will not tell. Okay?"

"Thank you." Julia glanced at Ford, still humming to himself with impressive musicality. "What about him?" she asked with a small smile, nudging her head in his direction.

Brynn's eyes flicked to Ford, who was obediently not paying attention. "He won't say anything, will you, Boy Scout?"

"About what?" he asked absently, pausing in his humming.

"Exactly." Impossibly, Brynn found herself smiling at him again, feeling oddly reassured that he would respect anything he'd overheard and keep things private.

She wasn't sure how she knew that, but she did.

As though Ford knew she was smiling, he looked at her in the rearview mirror again, and he was smiling, too.

There went her stomach again.

"Okay, here's my phone," Ford said suddenly, picking it up from the bucket seat and handing it over to Brynn. "Remember my passcode? 695847. Put your number in and text yourself, so you ladies can call me when you're ready to come back."

"We can get a cab," Julia insisted, turning around to face the front. "Really."

Ford looked at her. "Not many cabs in Lost Creek, ma'am. I'll be your ride."

"What if you're not done with whatever you're doing?" Brynn demanded without any of the agitation she thought her question would hold. "We don't want you to leave early."

"I'll have enough time," he assured her. "Put the number in."

Brynn gave him a look. "Ford . . ."

He met her eyes again. "If I'm not done, I'll say so. Cross my heart. You ladies can walk to Mariah's Cafe and Bakery—it's right there. Hang out until I'm there. I'll pay for it; I've got a running tab there."

"You have a tab at a bakery?" Brynn asked before she could help herself.

Ford smiled again, a soft laugh coming from him. "You haven't been to Mariah's yet, have you, Doc?"

Chapter 9

THERE WAS SOMETHING DISTRACTING about Brynn Kershaw. Maybe it was the deep honey color of her hair—the way it contrasted against her green eyes and seemed to perfectly drape along her shoulders. But it was in a ponytail today, so that couldn't be the excuse at the moment.

Maybe it was the way she smiled with her whole face when she wasn't controlling it, and a tiny, almost unnoticeable dimple appeared in her right cheek. But she hadn't smiled like that when Ford first met her, so he'd have only seen that recently.

Maybe it was how fantastic she looked in a pair of jeans and a T-shirt, which he had only seen today, and how having her hair pulled back didn't diminish any of her beauty. Or how perfectly she seemed to fit on the ranch, despite not being a ranch girl. Or how crazy hot it was to catch whatever her lotion or perfume was, mingled with the unmistakable scent of hay.

Whatever the reason, she was a distraction for Ford, even when she wasn't around him. His inability to manage under four seconds wrestling a steer was proof enough of that, and he absolutely could not blame the new hazers he was trying out at the arena. They'd all done a decent enough job of getting the steer where it needed to be for him, which left the rest of the work to him.

Should have been easy enough.

Except he was blowing it.

He hadn't had this much trouble practicing with Ryan and the guys back at the practice arena at the ranch, but out here at the official practice arena in Lost Creek, with guys who were on staff with the rodeo team at Sam Houston Community College and had professional experience in being hazers, he was just hopeless.

"One more," he grunted as he released the steer and got up, brushing himself off. "Tad, can you go again?"

"Got it," the guy replied, waving another handler forward with a steer. They got the steer situated in the chute while Ford got his horse back from the pickup man helping them out.

The practice arena outside Lost Creek belonged to Pete Weaver, a SHCC alum himself who was the chief supporter of the college's rodeo team. When Ford and the rest of the Original Six had formed the team, he'd immediately reached out to Coach and offered his ranch as training grounds. Now it was an official college athletics site, and was rented out regularly to other rodeo guys coming in for events.

Pete was a great guy, especially when it came to favors for SHCC rodeo alums.

Biting back a sigh, Ford got back up into the saddle and turned the horse back for their own chute. It didn't take him long to get into position, considering he wasn't going for full focus. He glanced over at Tad and the steer, getting a nod in return.

"Go!" Ford called.

Full Rigged

The chute opened, and the steer bolted, Tad and his horse riding perfectly alongside. They hadn't done the full setup with Ford's own barrier, so one of the other hazers called for him to start when the distance was about right. If they'd really been practicing, Ford would have asked for the full setup with ropes and barriers in the chutes to make sure every detail was right.

But he was testing out hazers today, so it was less about him at this point.

In theory.

Brynn was making everything more difficult.

There was no telling what would happen when he really needed to practice if this kept up.

"Haw!" Pete bellowed from behind him.

Ford jammed his heels into his horse's flanks as soon as the first hint of the yell sounded, and the well-trained horse bolted, streaking out of the chute and heading for the steer that Tad kept in line.

He felt the pounding of the horse's hooves as a cadence for his pulse, and his eyes narrowed as he neared the steer. He released the reins, and reached over just as they reached the steer's shoulders, taking the horns in hand.

He let the slowing steer pull him from the horse slightly, then threw his weight toward the ground, his feet digging in easily. Using his own motion, and that of gravity, Ford yanked hard at the horns and neck of the steer, throwing the animal off balance and toppling it to its side, feet flailing in the air.

"TIME!"

Ford patted the steer's neck, rubbing fondly. "Good boy. Hup." He pushed gently, prodding him to rise, which he did without hesitation. He wiped off his hands and looked at the others. "Well?"

Pete nodded with a slow smile. "Four-one, man. Not bad for a hazer test."

No, but definitely not something Ford wanted to make a regular thing.

He was better than that.

"You good?" Pete called as Ford got up. "Wanna go again?"

Ford frowned as he moved over to his things, part of him wanting to keep practicing, part of him wanting to get out of here. He could get more done with the guys back at the ranch than he could here, but there were other issues with being there. Reid would be coming back in late tonight, which meant there wouldn't be more practicing tonight, but tomorrow they'd all have to hit it hard. Reid was as driven as any of them, borderline obsessive, and he'd have kept practicing.

Unless a certain lady had other plans for him.

Interesting distraction, ladies.

He looked at his phone and his decision was made.

Done at the clinic. We'll be at the bakery. No rush.

The number must have been Brynn's, but she hadn't named herself in his phone. She'd just texted herself from it, which made him smile.

He'd used an old trick, and she had known it, but he hadn't meant it that way. He'd really been thinking only of convenience, but now she was in there . . .

"Nah, I'm good," he told the others. "Thanks, guys." He shoved his phone in his pocket and grabbed his keys, tapping his hat. "Okay if I jet? I've got to pick some people up, or I'd help with cleanup."

Pete waved him off. "We've got a few kids on the college team coming out to practice, so we'll just reset for them. Get out of here."

Ford nodded and saluted jauntily with a few fingers before making his way out to his truck. There was something about being back at this arena that made him smile. So many memories from his days at Sam Houston Community College, so many events they'd hosted on the official grounds up the road, and the echoes of the good and the bad both there and here at the training grounds all came back to him. Injuries, failures, disqualifications, and penalties had toughened him up, and victories had grown sweeter than he'd ever known. He'd learned about brotherhood and being part of a team, about fighting for a cause bigger than yourself, and how incredible it could be to cheer harder for someone than you'd ever be able to cheer for yourself.

This place, this town, was where he had learned the most about himself, and where he had become a man.

This was as much a home to him as the family ranch in Montana was.

He kicked at a bit of the dirt near his truck, smirking to himself.

What a great place.

His phone buzzed and he blinked, forgetting all about it in his nostalgia. He pulled it out and saw a message in The Chute, his group chat with the guys.

Strange how that made him a little disappointed.

Reid: *Y'all ready for me??? We're having steak, right?*

He opened the door of his truck and tossed his phone onto the passenger seat before climbing in. Someone else would respond, and Ford could react then.

Right now, he had something more important to do.

The drive to Mariah's was a short one, given that Lost Creek wasn't all that big, and the arena was its main attraction. The bakery combined the classic look of a building in an Old West town with a quaint hometown cafe, and really deserved a bigger premises for how popular it was.

Mariah was a kind woman in her thirties with a couple of

kids and a knack for any and all baked items. Pot pies, fruit pies, bread, cookies, turnovers, the works. She'd turned part of the place into a cafe in the last few years, and it turned out, the woman was just as good at soups and sandwiches as she was at cakes.

If she weren't already married, Ford might have made a play for her.

He'd also have accepted connections to any sisters or cousins she might have.

Except he was a little distracted at the present, and that distraction was sitting at a table in the place, looking out the window, a barely touched berry streusel muffin on a plate in front of her.

That was a sign of a problem if nothing else was.

Those muffins were a hot commodity. Ford had bribed Mariah shamelessly to have a box set aside for him to take to his mother, and she hadn't stopped talking about them since. It had been worth it, but Ford was pretty much in Mariah's debt for the rest of his life for that.

He pushed open the door to the bakery, the bell over the door jingling.

Mariah appeared from the door to the kitchen, smiling in greeting as she came to the counter. Her smile turned sarcastic when she saw him. "Oh, it's just you. Need something?"

Ford grinned at the jab. "Not today, but I will pay off my tab." He pulled his wallet out, opening it. "They did put it on the tab, right?" he asked, nudging his head toward Brynn.

"No . . ." Mariah frowned and looked at Brynn herself. "Dr. Kershaw, did you forget that Ford was footing this bill?"

"It's fine," Ford assured her, handing over his card anyway. "Ring it up, and just make up a punch card for her next visit or something. Julia, too."

Mariah didn't argue, taking his card and running the

transaction. "I don't have punch cards, Ford. We're not a chain."

He gave her a look. "Tell me you can't have your girls color something that your employees will know to honor."

The woman chuckled softly and shook her head. "Alrighty, I'll ask them to do something and send it to the ranch. Now go sit over there with the doc. She seems to have a lot on her mind."

Ford saluted, not needing to be told twice, especially since he already planned on doing exactly as she instructed.

Brynn didn't even look up as he approached, continuing to stare out the window at Main Street. Her position appeared relaxed, but her body itself didn't match that. Her back didn't touch the chair, she sat at the edge of the seat, and her hands gripped her folded arms rather than rested there.

A jolt of worry shot into the pit of Ford's stomach. Had something gone wrong at the clinic with Julia? He looked around the place, seeing a smiling, tearful Julia on the phone in a corner.

That looked promising.

Ford glanced down at Brynn again. "Can I sit here?"

She blinked, looking at him slowly. "Yeah, sure." She flicked her fingers toward the chair next to her.

He took it, watching her carefully. "Why'd you get the muffin if you aren't gonna eat it?"

"What?" She looked down at her plate, then seemed to wake up from whatever daze she'd been in. "Oh. Right." She smiled a little, looking at the muffin. "It looked too good to resist. Not even hungry, but had to get it." Her eyes flicked in his direction, but didn't quite meet his. The plate slid a little toward him. "You can have some."

Ford stared at it, then at her. "Maybe you should get yourself checked out, Doc. Nobody shares those."

"If you don't want it . . ." The plate started back toward her.

His hand snapped out to grip the edge of it, stopping the motion. "Didn't say that. Just thought you should know."

She shrugged. "Now I know." She pinched off part of the streusel crust on the top, popping it into her mouth. "And you don't have to call me Doc. I'm not here in any medical capacity. Just call me Brynn."

Ford bit back a smile at the invitation, trying for the casual air she was almost mastering. "Can do. Everything go okay over at the clinic?"

Brynn paused in her chewing. "Depends on what you wanted to hear. As with anything." She swallowed and cleared her throat. "Everything go okay with . . . whatever you were doing?"

He chuckled and reached out for part of the soft side of the muffin. "Good enough. And I was testing out hazers."

"What's a hazer?" Brynn asked, finally looking at him directly.

Her eyes really were amazingly green, and made her complexion seem like something in a painting of a sunrise.

That was just reaching for sappy, especially for him.

Didn't make it less true, though.

"I'm a steer wrestler," he explained, trying not to rush his words, as he needed to focus on something unrelated to her. "In the rodeo. Basically, I jump off a horse and take down a steer. Point is to get all the feet off the ground."

Her mouth quirked. "The steer's or yours?"

He squinted at her a little, catching the joke. "The steer gets a head start, and a rider launches with him, driving him in a nice line for the bulldogger." He paused, indicating himself with a hand. "Then I launch and chase after to take down the steer. You seen much of the sport of wrestling?"

"Some," she admitted with a shrug of a shoulder. "I have brothers."

"So you know a pin?"

She nodded once. "Put both brothers in a few over the years."

"It's kinda like that," he explained, loving the idea that this fairly petite woman was powerful enough to pin her brothers. "Steer has to be on its side, no feet touching. Fastest time wins."

"And you needed a new hazer?" she repeated, clearly thinking through what he'd said. "The one who basically keeps the steer in line for you?"

"Yep, my usual guy shattered his leg. Out all season."

Brynn made a sympathetic face. "Ouch. Big ouch. I may not get the event, but any sporting event with more than one person needs that team mentality and trust. So did you find your guy today?"

Now it was his turn to shrug. "Maybe. I might just ask Ryan to do it. He doesn't ride anymore with his injury, but I think he's itching to do something besides manage rodeo stuff."

Julia laughed on her call, drawing their attention. Ford smiled, having a pretty good idea what she was laughing about. Brynn, on the other hand, stiffened.

He gave her a look. "Hey, you okay?"

"Yep," she said tightly, the easy nature of the conversation they'd been sharing completely gone.

She didn't want to talk about it, that was clear, but Ford wasn't okay with how tense she'd gotten. She'd said at dinner the other night that she'd been angry since her husband's cheating, and something about lashing out, but was she really upset over whatever was making Julia laugh?

He'd admit to not knowing Brynn well, but he'd seen the

concern and care she'd taken with Julia on the drive in. She had a good heart; there was no way it could be that simple.

"I love you too," he heard Julia say, then watched as she hung up the phone, beaming from ear to ear. She looked over at them and waved a little, getting up and coming to them. "Sorry, guys. I'm ready whenever."

"No worries," Brynn said at once. "You needed to tell him, and talk things through. Sounds like he's happy?"

Julia nodded eagerly, smiling so widely her cheeks could have burst. "Yeah. He cried." She giggled, then looked at Ford. "I'm pregnant."

Ford smiled back. "Congratulations. And like she said earlier, I won't say a word. Let me know if you need pizza and pickles in the middle of the night. I can run out and get some."

"That's sweet." Julia paused, making a face. "And disgusting. Is that a normal one?"

"No clue," he replied. "My mom always said it was what she wanted when she was pregnant with me, so it's possible."

Brynn pushed back her chair and rose quickly. "Okay, let's head back to the ranch! I'm sure Kellie will want to chat, Jules, and Dr. Mills said he'd fax over the notes to her so you can have copies to take home."

Ford tapped a finger on the table near the muffin, getting ready to remind her of it, but the two ladies linked arms and started out of the bakery without it.

Hmm.

Grabbing a pair of napkins, Ford scooped up the muffin and started after them, dropping a few bucks in the tip jar on his way out.

They settled into the truck, Julia insisting on taking the back seat this time, and headed back toward Broken Hearts Ranch, none of them saying much.

"Ford, can I roll the window down?" Julia asked as they reached the town limits.

He looked at her quickly. "'Course. Feeling okay?"

She nodded, still beaming. "Yep. Just want a Texas breeze right now."

He chuckled and pressed the window lock button. "Have at it. I usually keep them locked so my dog doesn't get the same idea. Sherlock would hang his head out the window all the way from Montana, if I let him."

The two of them began a conversation about his dog then, but Brynn never said a word. No reaction, no contribution, no indication that she heard a single word either of them said.

Ford kept an eye on her, and the only shift in her he saw was her right hand tightening its grip on the hem of her gray T-shirt. She'd gouge a hole in it soon, if she wasn't careful.

Something had set her off. Was she fighting against some wave of anger? Was it distress? Bad memories? Some combination of all three?

Or did she resent being here at all?

He'd seen career burnout before, and it wouldn't surprise him if a doctor would feel it hard in this day and age. She could be a caring person and still grow to hate always being the person asked to do medical favors.

But even that didn't seem right. There was something eating at this woman beside him, and he didn't like how she'd retreated into it.

They pulled up to the homestead house on the ranch, and Kellie came out on the porch as Ford threw the truck into park. He got out to help Julia down, only to find her already heading up the stairs toward Kellie.

"Feeling better?" he heard Kellie ask, but he didn't hear Julia's answer as she hurried into the house.

He turned back to the truck to check on Brynn, only to find her standing there and making no move toward the porch. "Kellie, I need a walk." Her voice cracked at the end, her hand still gripping at the hem of her shirt.

Ford immediately looked up at Kellie, her reaction to the statement seeming crucial.

Kellie stared at Brynn steadily, not seeming particularly surprised. "Okay. Dinner's at six."

Ford turned back to see Brynn striding away, not looking at anyone else. He watched her go, then looked back at Kellie. "Should I go after her?"

Kellie swallowed, then met his eyes. "She'll be okay."

"That's not what I asked," he told her.

She said nothing, but her expression told him what he needed to know.

"Can you take care of my truck?" he asked, starting after Brynn.

"Yeah. Give her space, Ford."

He waved in acknowledgement, taking the warning as just that rather than a signal to stop. He'd have been safer to just avoid the situation altogether, but he'd been raised to look after women and make sure they were respected and safe. His sisters had given him good practice, and time around Kellie's guests had proven that he'd been raised right. Brynn was a tough, strong, stubborn woman, and he had no doubt she would be fine, whatever was going on, but that didn't mean she should have to be alone.

Particularly in the late afternoon on a Texas ranch she didn't know all that well.

He didn't need to stop her, hold her back, or try to help.

He just needed to keep an eye on her.

Someone should.

Kellie couldn't be expected to be everywhere at once, not when there were six other ladies in her program. She thought it was good for Brynn to take a walk, and that was good enough for Ford.

He'd just hang out a bit behind her while she did so and make sure she got back to the house fine.

Easy enough.

She walked pretty fast, her strides long and her pace quick down the gravel road away from the house. It was hard to tell if she was being intentional in her choice of path or just desperate to get away, but he walked behind her silently, hands in his pockets. He had no doubt she knew he was there, but as he made no attempt to catch up or interrupt in any way, she seemed content to let him follow.

Or she tolerated it, at any rate.

Brynn stopped in the center of the gravel road they were currently on, a strange ripple or shudder seeming to roll up from the center of her back. She suddenly turned and marched into the field to her left, then began to run.

Ford jogged after her, wondering what she was planning or where she thought she was going. Not that it mattered—she'd have to run for an hour to get off ranch property—but the sudden change worried him.

She suddenly began to yell—a hoarse, roaring sound that kicked him in the gut. She staggered to a stop, bending over with her hands on her knees, taking in a deep breath, then bellowing once more. The sound was so raw, so shattering, that Ford could hardly believe it had come from Brynn. Her body shook with the force of it, and she dropped to her knees as it began to waver in tone and strength.

If he never heard that sound again, he'd still never be able to forget the anguish in it.

He waited a distance away, heart pounding hard as though he had been the one roaring at the earth and sky. Would she yell again? Would she beat the ground with her fists? Would she scream and sob in distress?

Nothing seemed to happen for a few moments. There was no sound but the light breeze stirring the tall grass. Then

Brynn began to sway a little where she knelt, and he started toward her, afraid she would pass out.

But she only sniffed, a faint clogging sound in it the only indication of tears.

Ford paused, afraid to go closer, and just as afraid to leave.

"Well?" Brynn asked, not turning toward him. "I couldn't shake you off, which makes you the only person to have seen me go full surge. I'm not going to ramp up again for at least an hour—probably not at all. So you might as well say something."

The defensiveness in her tone didn't affect him so much as the defeated nature of it. This mute acceptance of something so overwhelming and clearly exhausting, this animal of an experience that drained her regularly enough to have developed a pattern she could identify.

None of this was okay.

Neither was it her fault.

"I'm just wondering if you want a hug," Ford called, careful to keep his voice as unaffected as possible. He didn't want to upset her one way or the other, and in an emotionally exposed state like this, there was no telling how she would react.

She whirled in place, staring at him in a sort of horror, her cheeks stained with tears. "Are you serious right now?"

He shrugged slowly and held his arms out a bit. "You're holding in a whole lot of hurt and anger to do something like that. And that kind of hurt and anger could probably use a hug. That's all I'm saying. Take it or leave it."

He held his breath, leaving his arms where they were, invitation waiting there.

Brynn stared at him, her eyes wide. Slowly, she pushed to her feet, eying him the way a wild horse might have done.

With her emotions on high alert, he supposed she was more like a wild horse than anything else, ready to bolt if given the chance and wary of everything and everyone.

He could work with wild horses. He had the patience to gain their trust and make them comfortable, to tame them into a creature of harnessed power and loyalty.

There was no telling if those years of training would work here with Brynn, but he'd try his luck.

She surprised him by coming toward him, her steps seeming a little less steady than before, her demeanor less determined. It only took a moment for him to realize that she wasn't slowing, and wasn't going to stop.

She was going to let him hug her.

The significance of the moment would never be lost on him.

Brynn exhaled shortly as she walked into his arms, her cheek resting against his chest as though it had done so before. He latched his arms around her, holding her tightly without crushing her, feeling the tremors that shook her frame as they now quivered into him.

He closed his eyes and forced his breathing to slow, keeping each inhale and exhale steady. Her rapidly flying heart pounded against the measured cadence of his own, and her slender arms eventually reached around him in return. Then, without warning, they cinched across his back and chest with an almost startling power as she began to gasp and moan with waves of sobs.

Ford returned the pressure, securing her against his chest with a firmness that he hoped would comfort and reassure her. She slumped against him, her knees buckling as she cried, but he held her still.

"It's all right," he murmured, gently lowering them both down and cradling her against him as he sat on the grass. "You're all right."

Brynn buried her face against him, sobbing uncontrollably, each one ripping through her and, consequently, through him.

He tightened his hold further still, as though he could pull her into his own chest and protect her there. "Let it out, Brynn," he told her, pressing his mouth against her hair. "Let it all out."

CHAPTER 10

IT WAS AMAZING HOW Brynn could think back on something that should have been the most embarrassing moment of her recent life and not actually feel embarrassed about it.

It was scary, actually.

She should be completely mortified that Ford had witnessed her go full surge, and that she'd then sobbed in his arms so long that snot had gotten involved. Full ugly cry, with blotchy face, swollen eyes, and mucus factory engaged.

The epitome of all embarrassing things.

But she wasn't embarrassed.

She was just exhausted. Mentally, physically, emotionally exhausted.

Walking with Ford helped, though. After she'd made a mess of herself and stopped shaking-slash-crying, they'd just sat in silence side by side, his shoulder touching hers. There was something just as comforting in the touch of his shoulder as there had been in the hold of his arms. Some deep, human connection that grounded her in a way nothing else had in the last year-and-a-half.

She wasn't alone. So long as she could feel that connection to Ford, she wasn't alone.

"You wanna walk?" he'd asked after a long stretch of silence as they sat.

She'd nodded, and they'd been walking ever since. Not toward the house as she'd expected, but in the same direction she'd been going, almost rambling along the gravel road they'd been on before.

But walking got rid of that connection, and she felt small and cold without it. So she'd walked right beside him, practically hovering as though he was her protector. Ford had earned big points for not moving away, and she'd nearly cried when he'd taken her hand. It wasn't romantic, at least not in the way that most first hand-holding experiences were. He didn't lace their fingers, and neither did she, and the hold they had on each other was fairly secure.

No stomach flipping, no butterflies, no skipping heartbeats.

It just felt . . . good.

Really good.

"It was Julia's pregnancy," Brynn said at last as they continued to walk.

Ford squeezed her hand gently. "You don't have to explain anything."

"I'm not explaining," she told him, relieved that there wasn't a single hint of irritation in her tone. And more relieved that she didn't feel any irritation. "I just need to talk."

He nodded, and said nothing else.

There was something sweet in his simple acknowledgment and lack of additional commentary.

"I was fine when I suspected she was pregnant," Brynn went on, swallowing a sudden lump in her throat. "I was fine when we were at the clinic, and when her pregnancy was confirmed. All of that was fine. Purely medical, and nothing I haven't dealt with on a regular basis. But as soon as she got on the phone with her husband . . ."

Her voice didn't just break then—it broke down. Tripped on a vocal rabbit hole. Fell down a flight of vocal stairs. Crashed into a vocal six-car pileup.

Died a painful, horrifying, gruesome vocal death.

There was no way Ford missed the catastrophe in her voice, but he said nothing, his hand still firmly holding hers.

"He was so happy," Brynn choked out. "I could hear him laughing and cheering through the phone. And then they were both crying, and I . . . I was happy for them. Who wouldn't be? And then I was angry. I was furious. Not at them, or at their baby, but at my life. At my marriage. At . . . *him*."

Bile rose in her throat, filtering into her mouth, and she pressed her tongue against her teeth as she debated doing something she hadn't done in at least nine months.

"At Trent," she spat, nearly gagging at the sound of his name in her voice. But she had to say it. Had to hear it. Had to stop avoiding it.

Had to face it.

Brynn took in a slow breath, and released it even more slowly, wishing it was as relaxing as it was supposed to be. "I wanted kids after a year of marriage. We had talked about them when we were dating and after we got engaged. They were always in the plan, and then suddenly they weren't. There wasn't time for them, or he was gone too much, or I was on call too often. Maybe next year, maybe when he got his promotion, maybe when I was home more."

She laughed bitterly, shaking her head. "He never wanted kids with me. He never wanted anything with me. I was never going to be a parent so long as he was around. Even if I had gotten pregnant, he wouldn't have changed. He'd have traveled just as much, sleeping with any female he found appealing, and have come home the hero, charming the kids just as much as he charmed everyone else. Maybe I should be grateful we never had any. Who'd want to stay with me when the greatest actor of all time was the other option? I'd have ended up alone anyway."

The pressure against her hand tightened further, and she closed her eyes as it did so.

"I am so mad at him," she confessed, heat coursing from each strand of hair down through the rest of her like a wave of fire. "Every minute of every day, I am furious. I think that's why I get these surges. Anger is my neutral setting now, and stress feeds on anger. Like gasoline on a spark. And then boom! I boil over. One of these days, I'll lose the limited control I have left and explode on some unsuspecting person who's taking too long to order a coffee."

Brynn opened her eyes and looked over at Ford, finding his attention steady on her. "That's not an exaggeration either. I could have gone postal on a lady in the airport the other day for doing that. I don't know what started the surge that day, but travel is always stressful. And I thought . . . I thought I might see Minimus. Sorry, that's my code name for him so I don't have to say his name."

Ford's mouth curved to one side in a crooked smile. "Fitting. Nicely done."

That was the first thing he was going to say in all of this? This guy was no Boy Scout—he was a freaking superhero.

She managed a weak smile for his comment. "I was scared to come here. I've been burying all of the stuff from the marriage and divorce with work and distractions, all of the baggage just getting tossed aside and ignored. I think all of that built up, and that's probably why I snapped at you, too. Just for trying to help with my suitcase. I'm sorry."

"Nothing to be sorry for," he told her, his smile gentling. "Even people who haven't been through what you have get irritated and cranky with traveling."

"Don't make excuses for me," she pleaded. "It only makes my guilt and shame worse."

Ford lifted a brow. "It's not an excuse. It's validation."

It was horrible to admit, but she hadn't expected a word like that to come drawling out of his mouth as easily as a "yahoo" might have done. Ford seemed like such a simple guy, and, at least at first, she'd expected that to mean not particularly well-educated or well-read. But the guy was full of surprises, so why shouldn't he understand concepts like validation and properly express them?

"Validation?" Brynn repeated, something feeling foreign about the word. "How do you figure?"

He nodded firmly. "Seems to me that you're just as mad that you get mad as you are about everything else. Him included."

"I am," she surprised herself by saying. "I hate it. I hate that I can't control it or fight it back. I hate that I'm still dealing with this when the divorce has been finalized for a year. I see people who are so happy with their divorce and they're taking the town by storm in celebration. I didn't want to celebrate my divorce, though I was perfectly happy to get rid of the trash legally. I wanted to curl up on my couch with ice cream and avoid everyone. My first three weekends officially divorced, that's exactly what I did."

"Is it supposed to be easy?" Ford asked quietly.

She could only shrug at that. "I just wish I could cope with this better. I was writing in the journal Kellie gave me last night, and I think I get angry as a defense mechanism. I think I hurt so much that anger is the fortress around the hurt to keep it from getting worse."

"Makes sense to me."

He wasn't supposed to agree with her problems, and she gave him an exasperated look.

He returned it without shame. "I'm willing to bet Kellie has talked to you about this, right? Cuz I think you should be angry. You've been through hell because of him—that's worth some anger."

Brynn shook her head. "But it's so much," she whispered. "And I can't control it."

"Yet." He smiled, shaking the hand he held gently. "I've seen Kellie help people through all kinds of things. You'll get there."

She tilted her head to peer up at him, almost suspicious of his confidence. "How do you know?"

"You want to get there. Seems to me that's the most important part."

Encouragement. Validation. Comfort.

Was there anything this guy didn't understand about what Brynn needed?

"I'm scared," she told him, surprised at how easily she could do so. "I'm scared of hurting again once the anger goes down."

He nodded in thought, looking ahead at something down the road. "Tell you what. When you get scared or hurt, you text me."

That startled her after the easy, companionable conversation they'd been having. "Why? So you can scare the monsters away?"

"No, although I'd be happy to try." He chuckled and pointed up the road. "So you can get this guy to come and make you feel better."

Brynn looked to where he pointed, and her eyes widened. "The small bear walking toward us?"

"That's Sherlock," he told her, laughing again. "He's about the size of a beanbag chair, and decently comfortable. Good listener. Doesn't judge. Puts up with a lot. I'll volunteer him for you."

They both pulled up as the dog reached them, and Brynn stared at the massive animal while Ford squatted down to greet him. "What kind of monster dog is that?"

Ford grinned up at her, cueing the standard stomach flip for her. "Neapolitan mastiff. He's kinda shy, but once he likes you, he kinda forgets he's not a lap dog."

Brynn smiled, reached out, and began scratching behind Sherlock's ear. The wrinkly-faced dog immediately began nuzzling toward her, panting a little with his tongue lolling out. "I haven't had a dog in years," she murmured. "Minimus hated them."

"All the more reason to make friends with Sherlock," Ford said simply. He rubbed the dog's back, patting gently. "He's fine with strangers, don't worry."

"He's just a love, isn't he?" Brynn gushed, sinking to the dog's level and bringing her other hand up to scratch along the other side of his face. "Aren't you? You're just a great, big ball of mush and love. All soft and gooey."

Sherlock groaned and licked his face, shifting farther toward Brynn, leaning farther and farther into her actions.

Brynn chuckled at his antics, her heart warming at his innocence and sweetness. There was nothing as tender and unfailing as the heart of a dog, and she needed that sort of heart in her life right now.

The dog's eyes met hers then, and something about their gentle depths brought her to tears. She scratched and rubbed at his ears and along his neck, before leaning against him herself in a comforting almost-hug.

Her eyes, however, turned to Ford.

He was watching her interaction with Sherlock fondly, his smile easy and soft, surprisingly open, and undeniably genuine.

She hadn't felt that anything in her life had been genuine in ages.

"He's perfect," she whispered, stroking the soft fur of the massive dog in slow, absent motions. "Think he'll be okay with being my on-call body pillow?"

Ford snorted a soft laugh. "You seein' what I'm seein'? He's melting like butter. I'll bet you twenty bucks that tomorrow, given the choice between the two of us, he'll go for you."

"I'll take it." Brynn smiled at him, an air of contentment settling in her chest. "So I text you when I need Sherlock."

"Yep." Ford dipped his chin in a fervent nod, his smile turning more crooked.

Brynn swallowed, her heart skipping just one beat. "What if I need another hug?"

The crooked smile softened, and he searched her eyes. "For that, you call me. Anytime, no questions asked."

"I can't keep you on-call as well," she told him as her stomach dropped and her throat clenched. "That's . . . that's not . . ." Her eyes began to burn, and she wasn't entirely sure why. Panic began to rise, her hold on Sherlock tightening.

"Hey."

She blinked, not realizing her vision had begun to cloud. "What?"

Ford reached out and put a hand on her arm, the pressure somehow giving her breath and life. "This isn't anything more than what it looks like. I don't pretend. I followed you out here to make sure you'd be okay. Nothing more. I offered you a hug because I didn't know what else to do, and I wanted to help. I've offered you full and unrestricted access to my dog because

Full Rigged

there's something special about sitting in quiet with a dog. And I'm telling you now that if you think I can help in any way when you are overwhelmed, when your anger surges, when those walls come down and you're a mess of hurt, you can call me. I'll go for another walk, I'll sit and listen, I'll give you a hug that could last for seven hours if you needed it to."

"Why?"

Ford squeezed her arm, entirely serious now. "Because you've been alone in this world of hurt, and you don't have to be anymore. You'll be working with Kellie, and that's going to do you a world of good. She's brilliant, and she's got a big heart. Doesn't mean it's gonna be easy, and I don't mind being there when you need a break."

If she weren't already snuggling the man's dog, she'd have hugged him again. As it was, she shook her head against Sherlock. "Are you for real, Boy Scout?"

His laugh was soft, almost a caress of sorts. "As far as I know. Is that honest enough?"

Brynn managed a smile that she didn't have to force. "Yeah. That's enough." She sighed and lifted her head off Sherlock, scrunching the folds of his wrinkled face in her hands. "I think it's time to go back to the house."

"We'll walk you," Ford said as he pushed to his feet.

"That's not necessary," Brynn protested, tucking hair behind her ear. "I'm guessing these houses are where you're staying? You're home, don't come back with me."

Ford shrugged, sliding his hands into his pockets. "Left my truck at the house. Might as well let you and Sherlock hang out a little while longer while I go get it. Care if I walk in the same direction with you?"

It was the cutest, most non-intimidating offer she had ever received from a guy in her life, and for that reason alone, she loved it. "Oh, why not?" she teased, standing up and wiping her hands on her jeans. "Sherlock probably needs a walk anyway."

"He always needs a walk," Ford grumbled, giving the dog a wry look. "Come on, boy." He whistled loudly and nudged his head in the direction of the house.

Sherlock darted off as though after a rabbit stopping in the field and looking back at them eagerly.

"Are we chasing him?" Brynn asked with a laugh.

Ford shook his head, smiling just a little. "Nope. He thinks dinner is that way."

"Rude!" Brynn whacked Ford across the chest without thinking. "What's going to happen when he gets there?"

"Kellie will give him something!" Ford laughed and raised his hands to block another potential blow "I'm not that mean."

Brynn exhaled in faux irritation, easily taking Ford's hand in hers just like before. "I'm not going to be able to eat dinner thinking of that poor, starving dog."

"Well, then I'll leave half of the muffin from Mariah's out on the porch for you," Ford said, blessedly not reacting to her taking his hand again. "You can have that when you get hungry."

She gave him a confused look. "The muffin?"

He raised a brow. "Don't tell me you forgot the muffin. I know you left it there, and now that I get a little bit more where your mind was, I'll allow it, but to forget it completely? Not okay. It's manna from heaven, and now I'll eat the whole thing myself."

"You brought my berry muffin?" She threw her head back and laughed, the perfection in that act beyond delightful.

"Our berry muffin," he reminded her softly. "You offered me some."

She beamed at him, wondering when this strange dream

she was having would end. "I did, didn't I? Guess I'm only entitled to half after all."

If her stomach had flipped at his smile before, it cartwheeled now. "You have a beautiful laugh, Brynn. It's a great sound."

"I haven't really laughed in a long time," she confessed. She shook her head, mildly amazed that there was no embarrassment in saying so. "I hope I laugh more soon."

"So do I."

CHAPTER 11

"Three-eight! Nice run. Ryan, you might have to do this for real."

Ryan glared at Lars as he turned his horse. "As opposed to that pretend round I just did?"

Lars waved a dismissive hand at him, turning his attention to Ford on the ground. "Feel better?"

"Tons," Ford grunted. He jumped up and brushed off his sleeves. "Best run I've had in weeks."

"Looked the best, too." Westin nodded in approval as he helped settle the steer.

"Settles it for me," Eric told the group, raising a hand. "Any of us can do it, sure, but nobody's reading Ford or the steer like Ryan is."

"That's because Ryan's been talking to only steers for more than a year," a new voice called.

They all turned to look before cheers broke out at the appearance of Reid Browning, returned from his other life in D.C. and looking like the poster boy for rodeo stars. But that was how Reid always looked: button-up shirt, jeans, boots, hat . . . All neatly dirtied so you'd know he didn't come from any given mall in Texas.

Anyone looking at him without knowing the truth would think he was all hat and no saddle.

Those who knew better weren't fooled by his appearance.

The guy was a beast of a bronc rider, and there was no messing around when he was there. It was one of the reasons they called him Chute Boss. Mostly behind his back, but occasionally to his face as well.

He shook hands with them all, coming over to lean on the fence. "Go again, Ford. I wanna check this out."

Ford shoved his thumbs into his back pockets. "What? Having Ryan as my hazer?"

Reid nodded, all business now. "Having Marty out when you guys gel like you do isn't something to sneeze at. Other guys can have hazers they draw out of a hat, but you work better when you trust your guy. So let's go again."

There was nothing to do except just that, and Ford and Ryan exchanged bemused looks as they moved back to the chutes. Reid was going to be some kind of epic rodeo coach when he was done with his time in the spotlight, considering he already coached his friends and teammates.

They went through three more rounds of practice, the times hovering right around the same mark of three-point-eight seconds. Ford didn't mind that he wasn't dropping time with his runs; that wasn't the point. He needed to know that Ryan could be as good as Marty had always been for him, if not better. He had a routine and pattern down when it came to steer wrestling, and he needed his hazer to be part of that, not just jump in when he had a need. He might have been the one with his name on the board, but he'd always considered Marty his silent partner in the event.

Other steer wrestlers felt differently, and he was well

aware of the fact. But this worked best for him, and he was not about to change it now.

The more they practiced, the more it looked like Ryan would be his guy

Which was convenient, since the whole Lost Creek Days shenanigans started in a few days. Three nights of rodeo at the end of eight days of jam-packed activity to celebrate the town. It was an exhausting schedule, particularly since he and the other guys had been asked to be as visible as possible this year to help with publicity and attendance. The different rodeo events Lost Creek had put on in the last few months had helped to increase numbers, which had dwindled in recent years, but they wanted more.

Ford didn't mind, so long as no one made him give a speech or put on a stupid costume.

"Can someone else take a turn doing something now?" Ford finally asked as he sat in the dirt after a run, the steer already up and moving away. "I'm not the only one competing next week."

"Seriously," Ryan said from his saddle, leaning his forearms against the horn. "We're the only two breaking a sweat. Lars, let's set up some saddle bronc for you. Rocket's dying for a turn with you."

Lars immediately rubbed his hands together. "That nag? He's got nothing."

Reid gave Lars a bewildered look. "Tell that to the goose egg I got from him three weeks ago. Fifty bucks says Grandpa here is icing his backside in an hour."

"A hundred," Ford and Eric said together.

Westin snorted a laugh and hopped onto the fence. "This is gonna be good."

Ford had to agree. There was something invigorating about the six of them being together, bantering the way they usually did. They all drove each other to be better, but there was also no one who could get a rise out of them better than each other. Some of the best insults he'd ever heard in his life, as well as some of the most stinging ones he'd received, had come from these guys.

It was just the way they were. A ragtag bunch of cowboys that had become a family, with all the fun and spats that came with it. They laughed, they argued, they fought for each other, they teased each other, and they ultimately made each other better men and better athletes.

Nothing could be better.

After watching Lars fall on his rear twice, much to their amusement, and after money had exchanged hands, they got down to business. Lars and Reid had some great rides, West took on a few of the bulls and owned it, and Eric put them all to shame with some fantastic roping. Ryan acted as coach, as pickup man, as whatever they needed him to be. Ford kept an eye on him, wondering if being this involved without taking a turn himself was hard.

But Ryan never so much as flinched at any of it, apparently accepting of his new position and limitations without resentment.

It hadn't always been that way, and Ford was glad to see the change.

It was like having the old Ryan back.

It also meant that West wasn't going to get an inch of sympathy from him, given Ryan had competed in bull riding himself, so he had a vested interest in West's technique and success.

Poor guy.

After they'd had enough, they headed out of the practice arena to help Ryan with whatever needed to be done on the ranch that day. It was part of their way of paying rent while they stayed on the land, given Kellie and Ryan never let them stay in town like other rodeo guys. They always insisted that they stay in one of their ranch cabins or in their trailers on the land rent free.

Or, in Westin's case, park his truck on their land and sleep under it.

West was weird like that.

"What are we doing today?" Reid asked, clearly pumped up to get going on whatever it was.

Eric laughed once. "Too much D.C. in your blood? Need some dirt and grime?"

Reid nodded without shame and clasped his hands together. "Yes. Please."

"Ryan, do you have something that can get all that city slicker off of Reid?" Eric called up ahead of them, where Ryan had stopped.

He nodded, grinning. "I think I can come up with something. We've got a couple of things going on today, actually. Lost Creek Days starts tomorrow with the races, the carnival, and the Miss Lost Creek pageant. We haven't been asked to do anything, but I kinda volunteered us to take the ranch guests, if you don't mind. One of them in particular is really skittish with men, so she might not go, but if she does, we'll need to stick close."

They all sobered at once and Ford nodded. "Josie. I can stick with her, if she's comfortable with that. She was pretty scared of me that first day."

"That's because you're the size of a refrigerator," Westin told him with a snort.

Ford gave him a look. "I'll remember that next time you ask to borrow a shirt, Tiny."

Westin grinned and tapped his hat. "Touché."

"As for today," Ryan went on, "my cousin Holt is coming

in with some stock we'll be hosting until the stock auction on Thursday. If we could get the barn and stables cleared out and ready for extra animals, it would help a lot. When he gets here, I could use a few of you to get the animals settled and run them around a bit. I've got ranch employees working out on the land today, so this is pretty much our priority."

They all nodded, knowing the drill and understanding all too well what would be required.

Ryan glanced in the direction of the homestead house, then back at them. "I think a few of the guests are going to be in our neck of the woods. The one Ford and I mentioned, Josie, is going to feed the horses. It's her first day of chores. She hasn't felt ready yet. She already knows me, so I'll take point, but keep an eye out—no telling if it's a good day or bad."

This was also something they'd become familiar with. In the last few months especially, as they'd been in and around Lost Creek a lot, they'd met several of the guests at the ranch. Some of them had been far along in their healing and recovery journey, others at the very beginning.

Ford, for one, felt pretty protective of any guest staying at Broken Hearts, and he didn't see that changing anytime soon.

What would Brynn be doing today?

He gnawed the inside of his lip as the thought flashed through his mind. Their walk last night had been humbling and exhilarating for him, in several ways, and he'd had trouble sleeping as he'd gone over each part of it. Had he helped her with her hurting and angry outburst? Had their conversation lifted any of her burden? Did she trust him as much as he wanted her to?

Was she thinking about him as much as he was thinking about her?

A shard of guilt slashed across his chest, making him hiss

softly. There were so many different feelings where she was concerned, personal hopes and wishes that conflicted with the respectful distance he'd always given Kellie's guests. His concern for an obviously hurting woman was shifting into something less charitable and more affectionate. Less altruistic and more selfish.

He didn't like it.

And yet . . .

"Any other guests hanging out on our side?" Westin asked. "I want to see what Brynn asks Reid."

Ford grinned along with the others, while Reid looked confused.

Ryan laughed as well. "I don't know who's doing what; Kellie manages that. She gave me a heads up on Josie just because of the situation. It's a big deal for her to come out and do anything without a buddy. But she wants to try."

"Poor kid," Lars murmured with a shake of his head. "Sounds like it could be an abuse situation."

There were a few nods at that, and Ford felt a surge of protectiveness as well as a jolt of nausea at the thought. The same impulse to offer a hug rose up within him, but it didn't have the same reasoning as he'd had with Brynn. That had been helplessness mingled with particular interest and concern.

This made him feel like an angry big brother who wanted to hold his sister until the monsters were gone.

Ryan reached into his back pocket to pull out his phone, glancing at the screen. "Huh. Meteor shower tonight. Kells wants us to set up one of the fields for everybody to watch. We're invited, too, and she said she'll bring us dinner if we do." He looked at them all for their answer.

"Done," Ford said at the same time the rest gave their affirmative answers.

They'd do pretty much anything for food, especially if Kellie was the one making it.

Ryan sent off a quick response, then tucked his phone away. "Better get started, then."

Ford opted to work on the stalls, joined by Westin and Lars, and they began mucking out each of them quickly. The horses were out in the pen behind them, and it wasn't long before a small woman with mousy brown hair stood at the fence, staring at them wide eyed.

"Heads up," Westin said softly, nudging his head toward her.

They waited, looking for Ryan to appear beside her.

When he didn't, Ford started out slowly, eying her cautiously. "Josie?"

She jumped, attention shooting to him at once. She swallowed and gripped at the fence without a word.

"Hi," he said simply, keeping his distance. "Remember me?"

She nodded quickly. "Brynn calls you Boy Scout. She says you're okay, and I can trust you. I'm not . . . very good with that."

Ignoring the jolt of pleasure he felt at hearing Brynn's praise, Ford smiled. "That's okay. I'm not much of a people person. Are you here to feed the horses?"

Again, she nodded, looking about ten years old.

"Ever been around horses?"

She shook her head.

His smile spread. "Kinda makes it hard to feed them, huh?"

Her mouth curved in the smallest smile known to man, but Ford would call it a victory. "Yeah."

"Well," he said slowly, "I can bring a horse over to meet you, if you'd like. Got a couple of friends with me in the barn here doing chores, and they could do the same. One at a time. Don't need all the horses in your face, right?"

"Yeah," she said quietly, her voice shaking just a little, but the smile still there. "One horse at a time would be good."

They weren't talking about horses, and they both knew it, but the comparison worked as a good conversation piece without triggering Josie.

"Ryan will be here in a minute, I'm sure," Ford explained as he stepped out of the barn and shifted toward the horses rather than toward Josie. "He'll show you the ropes, so we'll just help you meet the horses until he shows up. If you want to."

"I do," Josie told him firmly, her voice the strongest he'd ever heard it. "Please."

He nodded, and went to the nearest horse, free of reins or saddle, gently nudging it toward her. He clicked his tongue, patting the horse's neck, as they walked together. "Josie, hold your hand out over the fence. She'll be curious and come over to you to sniff it out. Kinda like a dog. Ever had a dog?"

Josie nodded with a bigger smile. "I love dogs. Brynn introduced Sherlock to me after breakfast. He's the best."

"So that's where he was," Ford mused, not bothering to hide his delight at the mention of Brynn again. "Traitor. Glad you like him. This girl's just a little bigger than Sherlock, but it's a close call, right?"

"Right."

He stopped a bit away, letting the horse close the distance between them on her own, and smiled as Josie had a moment with her. For all her fear around men, there wasn't much hesitation with the horse, even with the size.

There was something both sad and sweet about that.

A faint hissing sound met Ford's ear and he glanced toward the stalls. Westin and Lars stood there, clearly having heard the conversation and watching with interest. Westin motioned lightly to the horses, and Ford nodded.

"Josie," he called over. "You okay to meet another one?"

"I think so," she replied without any concern. "I love this one, though."

He chuckled. "She'll be back when you have food, don't worry." He came forward just enough to pat the horse and nudge her along, grateful she made him look good by doing as he asked. He met Josie's eyes once the horse passed between them. "Westin is going to bring another one over, okay?"

She nodded, the smile fading a little, but not entirely. "Okay."

Ford moved back over to the barn, exhaling when he reached Lars. "I wasn't sure that was going to work," he admitted in a low voice.

Lars shook his head slowly. "It's amazing what Kellie's doing here for women just like her. Absolutely amazing. There should be a bigger house. We should bring in more of them . . ."

"You'd need another Kellie to do that," Ford pointed out, skipping over his use of the word *we*. "More people need more help, and Kells can't do everything."

"Right," Lars murmured in thought, seeming to be only half-listening. "Right." He shook himself and his eyes focused on something in the distance. "Here's Ryan. I'm gonna take my turn bringing a horse to Josie first, though. I don't want to miss out." He strode out of the barn toward the other horses.

Ford smiled at that and took the chance to pull out his phone, opening up the texts and starting a new one.

Heard Sherlock made an appearance this morning. Told you he liked you best.

He sent it off and laughed to himself as he saw the smile on Westin's face as he led his horse companion away from Josie.

"Meeting the horses, huh?" Ryan said when he came up to her. "That's great. Sorry I'm late, Josie. I didn't expect you for a bit longer."

Amazingly, she didn't seem all that flustered by having Lars and the horse to her front and Ryan at her left. Neither stood especially close to her, but there could still be the perception of crowding for someone with hypersensitivity.

But Josie was fine. Rubbing the horse's nose and smiling as though she hadn't a care in the world, she looked up at Ryan. "That's okay. I'm ready to get started."

Ryan grinned as though he had been the one helping Josie through her therapy and not his sister. "Then let's do it."

Ford's phone buzzed in his hand, and he glanced down at it.

Brynn: *He likes hugs, just like I do. Thanks for following me last night. You have no idea how much I needed that. Are you going to watch the meteor shower tonight?*

If he'd had any other plans, they'd have all been cancelled now.

Yeah, I'll be there. You?

He held his breath, watching the three dots move across the screen while she typed a response.

Brynn: *Yeah. See you there! I'll bring Sherlock.*

There was no helping the explosion of heat in his chest at that text, nor the stupid grin that crossed his face.

"What are you smiling at?" Westin demanded when he reached him. "What's happening?"

There were a ton of things happening, but Ford wasn't about to tell him anything.

He only shrugged and tucked the phone safely in his pocket again. "Mind your own business. Let's get back to work."

CHAPTER 12

BRYNN SAT OUTSIDE ON the porch steps, shaking and queasy, the breeze highlighting the path of tears on her cheeks. She wasn't sure if she was still crying; her face had lost feeling after her session.

It was the first time a surge hadn't been angry.

The residuals of it were almost as unsettling as the surge itself had been.

She'd run from the house when it happened, and Kellie hadn't followed. That was a relief, given the processing she'd had to do.

The walls were coming down, Kellie had said. That's why this surge was feeling different. They weren't gone, but they were coming down.

It was supposed to be a good thing, and yet it felt terrifying. She was so exposed, so open to injury and feeling, so unprotected.

Her anger had protected her.

She wanted the anger gone, but she wanted the protection back.

Could she have both?

"Hey."

Kellie's soft voice came from behind her, and Brynn didn't turn. "Hi," she replied on a long sigh.

"Can I sit?"

"Are you going to ask me more questions?"

"Nope."

"Then you can sit."

Kellie did so, folding her arms and resting them on her knees as she sat beside her. She looked out at the land in front of them, the Texas breeze picking up a few strands of her blonde hair and waving them in the air.

Brynn sat silently, her heart pounding in her chest with the strangest desire to talk to this woman, despite what had just happened.

Despite breaking down and nearly having a panic attack.

Despite aching everywhere.

Despite feeling like she'd been sunburned on the inside of her chest.

She wanted to talk to Kellie.

"I'd distanced myself from my dad's behavior," Brynn admitted with a faint sniff. "It had been part of my life for so long, I never took the time to associate his cheating on Mom with Minimus cheating on me. I can tell you with perfect clarity everything about the day my dad walked out. I know which girlfriend he was moving in with, and I can tell you the exact perfume she wore because he smelled like it. But I can't tell you what Mom's cries sounded like at night. She did cry, I remember that, but I've lost the sound. It's just a fact in my head. He left; she cried."

"You were a kid," Kellie murmured softly. "Kids block things; kids protect themselves from pain. You needed to forget the sound to protect your own pain. Crying is fine, and you have to let yourself do that."

Brynn bit her lip. "Did my blocking her crying keep me from feeling I could cry? I mean, I do cry, and I did cry, but it wasn't my default setting. Did I do this because of my dad?"

"You're going to have to explain what you mean by 'do this' a little more," Kellie told her, keeping her voice gentle. "Otherwise I'll have to ask questions, and I said I wouldn't."

It was almost enough to make Brynn laugh, but she was still too raw. "Did I bring these surges upon myself by somehow, subconsciously, telling myself not to cry about it?"

Kellie exhaled slowly and reached a hand out to take Brynn's. "That's a tough one. The answer is maybe. It doesn't mean it was wrong. You coped with your father's infidelity and abandonment in the best way you could with the resources you had. It could be that something as simple as the sound of your mom crying was so horrible for you that it put up that first wall for you. That first protection."

Brynn nodded, swallowing hard. "And yet I found a guy exactly like him, and I've followed the same pattern. It's like that cycle of abuse, right? Some children whose fathers were abusive wind up in abusive relationships. I should have been smart enough to notice Trent was the same sort of cheating scum. I should have seen the way he looked at other women for what it was. I should have listened to the insecure voice in my head the entire time. She was right, and I shut her up and told her she was being silly."

"It won't do you any good to beat yourself up for believing what you wanted to believe," Kellie said firmly, squeezing her hand hard. "Or what he wanted you to believe. Manipulative people get away with being manipulative because they are good at it. That's not a weakness on your part. That's just them. Not you. Them."

It was a nice thing to say, but not easy to believe. Brynn was the one who was here at this ranch because she couldn't function as a normal human being. She was the one needing to escape at random times to yell at the sky or, like today, have a near-breakdown without her defensive anger to protect her.

She should have been better than all of this. She should have been smarter. More equipped.

Above the noise.

But here she was, sunk down in the middle of it, unable to face her own emotions.

"You are not a victim, Brynn."

Something about Kellie's words in such a calm tone rippled through Brynn, and the simple statement sank into her chest with a firmness that rooted her in place.

"I am not a victim," Brynn repeated softly, her eyes widening. She looked at Kellie, startled by the freedom in the statement. "I'm not, am I?"

Smiling gently, Kellie shook her head. "Nope. You're not. And you called your ex by his name just a minute ago without a pause. Giving him a name makes him just another face in a crowd. Nothing to avoid, nothing to fear, nothing to tick on your radar. Just a man."

Brynn laughed breathlessly, wiping at her cheeks finally. "I always wanted to make him smaller and put him in this tiny box. Make him insignificant. It never occurred to me that changing his name would actually give him significance instead."

"Isn't that amazing?" Kellie rubbed Brynn's hand, pride and warmth radiating from her. "Our instinct to wipe them from our lives just makes them a stain. Thinking of them just like we would think of anyone else is the best way to make them smaller. To make them less of a trigger."

"Anything that reminds me of him is bound to set me off," Brynn admitted as she drew her knees closer to her chest. "How do I stop that? I don't want to always think of my life now as post-him. I just want it to be my life."

Kellie released her hand and turned on the porch to lean against the railing post. "There's no one way to do it. You just have to decide that you aren't living your life in a post-him era. You are living. You need to find fulfilling things to fill your day, things to look forward to, ideas to ground you. And you need to be gentle with yourself, and patient with yourself. What you have endured is hard. It challenges every single person who experiences it. There is no immediate recovery. It is a day-to-day process. But you have the power to decide the tone of each day, and which era you want to live it in. You are not a victim."

Brynn nodded, the tightness in her chest loosening at the reminder. She smiled almost ruefully at her therapist and friend. "You're really good at this, you know."

That made Kellie laugh and smile herself. "Hey, thanks!" She looked out at the lands of the ranch again. "I don't pretend to have all of the answers, Brynn. Not even close. I'm still healing myself in a lot of ways. I still live day to day. All I'm trying to do here is give people some tools and direction to help themselves start to live whatever the new version of their life happens to be."

"It's fantastic," Brynn said without hesitation. "We're all trying to heal, and we're similar in some ways, but so different, too. But we all need to heal, and that's our unifying trait. We're all broken. You're also creating a new empathy within us for all of the other broken people we're going to meet in our lives."

Kellie glanced back at her, smiling softly. "You're going to make me cry."

"Crying's fine, remember?" Brynn grinned with surprising ease, given her recent emotional cacophony. "You deserve some validation for what you're doing here, and all the effort you're putting in. All the good you're making possible. Look at Josie. She couldn't even look at a man when she got here, and now she's feeding horses with Ryan and who knows who else."

"Josie's come a long way on her own," Kellie said at once. "She's an eager student, but she's also got a tough road ahead. I'm just helping her find what works for her."

Brynn gave the woman an exasperated look. "Stop deflecting my validation."

Kellie laughed again. "Where'd you pick up so much passion for validation?"

The question made her pause, but then she managed to smile without blushing. "Ford."

Her friend's eyes widened. "Ford?" She leaned her head back against the post, seeming torn between a smile and a frown. "Ford's a great guy. You're not going to find anybody as low-key yet loyal." Her focus intensified on Brynn. "Do you like him?"

Brynn coughed at the directness, her face flaming now. "I barely know him . . . He was very sweet in that surge I had last night, and he's a breath of fresh air after Minimus, but he . . . I . . ." She squeezed her eyes shut and fought down the rising panic. "He's a really good-looking guy who makes me feel less broken. I don't know what that means, but that's all I can safely admit."

Kellie was silent for a moment, which was convenient, as waves of crashing sounds filled Brynn's ears as the war within her waged.

Don't fight your emotions. Acknowledge them. Don't resist. Accept.

A gasp escaped Brynn, and as she let go of her hastily placed barriers, she found the tide of emotions less turbulent than she'd expected.

When she was finally free of all the internal noise, Brynn exhaled slowly, shakily, and looked at Kellie in elated victory. "I did it."

"Yes, you did," Kellie agreed, looking as pleased as though she had fought the battle herself. "I'm sorry I sent you there with my question, though. I wasn't trying to test you. I care about both Ford and you very much, and I just want to make sure that you're able to heal the way you need to, and that he is respecting that."

Brynn smiled at the concern. "It's Ford, Kells. He's the Boy Scout, remember? You're telling me you think he'll be a problem?"

Kellie paused, considering that. "Point taken. Alrighty." She slapped her thighs and pushed to her feet. "Let's get dinner going and get things ready for the meteor shower in a few hours."

"I'm a terrible cook," Brynn warned as she got up. "You might regret this."

"Can you chop, Doc?" Kellie asked with a teasing smile. Her brow suddenly creased as she focused on something behind them. "What in the . . .? Is that Sherlock?"

Brynn clamped down on her lips and looked behind her. Sure enough, the massive gray dog was loping toward them. "Yeah . . ."

They watched as the dog approached them and stopped by Brynn's side, looking up at her.

Kellie looked at Sherlock, then back up at Brynn. "Interesting." Her mouth curved in a smile and she turned to go into the house, leaving Brynn no choice but to follow.

She looked down at the dog helplessly. "Timing, buddy. We gotta work on your timing. Come on."

Hours later, Brynn and the other guests were headed out to the field designated for watching the meteor shower, piled into the back of Kellie's newly-fixed truck. The sun had just barely gone down, leaving the evening cooler, which had all of them in jackets or sweatshirts over whatever they'd worn earlier in the day.

All of the guests had come, even Josie. She was pretty quiet, but assured them all she was feeling better than she had in days.

For someone as introverted as Josie, spending a chunk of the day with men had to be draining, and given her fears, twice as difficult. The fact that she was coming out with them tonight after a day like that was huge, and a significant sign of her progress in just a few days.

Brynn could only wish for such progress herself.

She hadn't texted Ford again after their morning exchange, though she'd thought about it at least four times after the breakdown in her session. She'd kept telling herself that there was no point in texting him more when they'd established they'd be seeing each other tonight, but it hadn't stopped the impulse from recurring.

She'd manage to quiet it, though. By looking up videos of Ford on the internet. Plenty of steer wrestling videos, which made her wonder just how dumb and/or crazy the guy was, and enough of them that she had a fair idea just how good he really was at the insanity.

He was very good.

And she'd watched enough to actually understand a little bit about the event itself, which would prove useful when they went to the rodeo at Lost Creek Days next week.

But the best video Brynn had seen hadn't been a rodeo video at all, unless you counted the fact that it was posted on Eric's channel, which bore the name of Rodeo King.

It had been one of the earliest videos on the channel, part of a series Eric had posted about the life of cowboys, and this particular video had Ford sitting at a campfire with a guitar and a cute blonde teenager. Expecting just another wannabe cowboy singing a lukewarm country song, Brynn was startled to find that Ford was a fantastic guitar player and a better than average singer, and the girl singing with him managed an almost eerily perfect harmony. It wasn't a show-off kind of song for either of them, more bluesy than country, and more bluegrass than bluesy. Some hybrid of all three genres, maybe, but the perfect song for sitting around a fire.

There weren't nearly as many views on this video as the others on Eric's channel, and Brynn could not see why. This was some serious talent, something special, and she'd found herself a little breathless and almost teary when it ended.

She'd definitely wanted to text Ford after that, but resisted.

Now they were heading out to the pasture for the meteor shower, and she felt more anxious than she had for most of the dates in her life.

Which was strange, as this wasn't a date.

Or, if it was, it was the biggest group date she'd been on since she was fifteen, and the numbers would be skewed.

She wasn't sure what she'd feel when she saw Ford again. Would she be excited to see a familiar face? Or embarrassed from the mess of the last time they were together? Would her stomach flip at his crooked smile? Or would she see just her new friend and on-call hug buddy?

Before she could worry herself into a knot, the truck pulled to a stop behind a line of three other trucks, and she heard the laughter of little kids.

She looked out at the field, bewildered by it. "Who's got kids?"

"Caleb does," Julia told her with a quick grin as she dropped the tailgate for them all. "Two or three, I can't remember. They must be staying up for the meteor shower."

Now this definitely wasn't a date.

Which was good.

She didn't want to go on a date with Ford.

She stumbled a little as she moved toward the tailgate to get down, her face flaming. Of course, she didn't want to go on a date with Ford! She didn't want to go on a date with anybody! She was so against dating right now that it wasn't even funny, and the idea of finding romance ever again . . .

Brynn frowned at herself as she hopped down. She was supposed to feel panic at that, maybe even a full surge worth. But she hadn't.

She wasn't panicked, and she definitely wasn't surging. Weird.

"Hey, dinner!" Ryan called out when he caught sight of his sister. "What do we get?"

Kellie snorted as she got out of her truck. "If I know you guys, you ate already, and this is second dinner."

"So what if it is?" Westin demanded from the blanket he sat on, several others scattered out around him. "We've worked up an appetite today!"

"I'm sure you did," Kellie replied without any concern. She hefted a laundry basket of wrapped food. "Tinfoil dinners, boys. Kellie style."

Confused expressions looked back at her, except from Ryan.

He was grinning like an eight-year-old. "Seriously, Kells? Don't tease me."

"Not teasing," she quipped, sending one of the dinners out to him like a frisbee. "Travels well, tosses nicely. What else do you need?"

"Not a dang thing!" he called back, sitting on his blanket and digging in.

Brynn watched as Kellie deftly tossed the other dinners out, even sending some over to Caleb and his wife, and the heavenly aroma of barbecue and meat filled the air.

Even though she wasn't hungry, Brynn's stomach rumbled from the smell.

She distracted herself by looking around for Ford as the other ladies moved toward open blankets. A hulking dog with a wagging tail caught her attention, and she sent up a silent prayer of thanks. Sherlock was better than a neon sign at the moment, and he was very interested in Ford's tinfoil dinner. Brynn moved in that direction, slipping her hands into the pockets of her hoodie and smiling without much effort.

"Hey," she said when she reached them.

Sherlock was instantly next to her, no doubt hoping she had a dinner to share with him. She rubbed his head before looking over at Ford, who hadn't moved.

"Hey yourself," Ford replied after a swallow.

Brynn gestured at the blanket. "Anybody sitting here?"

Ford looked at it, then smiled up at her. "Sherlock was, so . . ."

She snorted a laugh and looked at the dog. "Care to share, bud?"

Sherlock groaned, licking his face quickly.

"That means yes," Ford assured her, scooting over a bit. "Have a seat."

Brynn did so, leaning back and looking up at the few stars now winking above them as the daylight faded. "Are the stars amazing out here?"

"Yeah," he said without hesitation. "I mean, I'm from Montana, and I've never seen stars like what we get on the ranch up there, but it's pretty impressive here."

"Montana?" She brought her gaze down and focused on him. "That's pretty far from Texas."

He nodded, his smile soft and crooked. "Yeah, but I was just there, so it's fresh in my mind. Summer in Montana is gorgeous."

"Truth," Lars echoed from a few blankets away. "My favorite was always Christmas in Montana, though."

"Oh, yeah." Ford lay back on the blanket, peering up at the sky. "The most amazing sight is driving out at night. The sky is black because there are no cities close enough to lighten it." He spread his hands out, gesturing across the expanse above them. "Stars are everywhere, and then you see a ranch house in the distance. There's nothing else around, and everything is so clear. So clear, you can see the lights of their Christmas tree when there is no other light anywhere."

No one said anything for a moment, the entire group listening to Ford talk. Brynn, for one, was transfixed. She didn't have anything like that to share from childhood memories or of her home. She'd never felt so sentimental, or so connected to anything.

But something about hearing Ford share his memories filled that void a little, brought her a little comfort, just as he had done the day before.

How could he do that without even trying?

Ford lowered his hands, resting them on his chest and shaking his head. "That's still my favorite thing about Montana, honestly."

"I forgot that," Lars murmured quietly, his voice harder to hear. "It was always so cool."

Everyone was silent again, the image striking even in the mind.

Then one of the other guys cleared his throat. "Was that before or after your face froze off?"

They all laughed at that, and Brynn found herself comfortable enough to lay back on the blanket fully, Sherlock settling between her and Ford with a groaning snuffle.

Ford glanced at his dog, chuckling and scratching at his ear. "Make yourself comfortable, why don't you?" His eyes moved to Brynn, and his smile made her stomach drop through her spinal cord. "How was your day?"

It was on the tip of Brynn's tongue to say "fine," but Kellie's rule about the word came to mine, and she opted instead for honesty. "Hard."

"How so?" he asked in a low voice. "What happened?"

"Therapy," she said simply, smiling with what she hoped was comfort. "It's okay, I think we've made some progress, but wow, was it raw. You ever feel like you've worked out so hard that you can feel every single muscle in your body? And then you still have stuff to do in your day?"

Ford grunted a soft laugh. "Yeah. I played hockey for a lot of years, and there's a few of those types of practices that stick in my mind."

"Of course, you played hockey. It's my favorite sport. Anyway, that's how I'm feeling." She shook her head, moving her hand to touch Sherlock's head for comfort. "All on the inside, but still. I don't ache everywhere, but . . . I can feel everywhere. Like a sunburn. Does that make sense?"

"Yep." His fingers crossed over to take hers, making her catch her breath. "I'm sorry it was raw, but I'm glad you think it's progress."

Brynn's chest tightened, but not with panic, and she let her fingers brush against his for a minute. "Do you always know what to say, Boy Scout?"

He laughed again, this time as his thumb brushed across her index finger. "Nope. Almost never. I usually don't say much, which lessens the chance of saying the wrong thing."

"You're on a good streak with me." She smiled, rolling her head over to face him fully. "I looked you up, you know. Videos, anyway."

"Oh boy." He exhaled playfully, his smile still gorgeous. "What'd you find?"

Brynn laughed to herself. "Steer wrestling, of course. You're nuts."

"I've heard that."

"But also guitar." She shook her head a little. "You're amazing."

How he shrugged lying flat on his back, she didn't know, but he did. "I'm all right. Didn't know that was on there."

"Eric's channel," she explained. "It was an old one; you were playing at a campfire." She paused, biting her lip. "With a cute girl singing beside you."

"My sister," he said quickly. "Shay. You want talent, she's got it in spades."

Of course he'd take the chance to praise his sister instead of himself. Of course he would.

"It was beautiful," she whispered, latching her fingers around his briefly. "I wish there were more videos of you doing that."

"I don't play for attention," he replied, matching her tone. "But anytime you want to hear something, you let me know."

Brynn swallowed hard at the sweet offer. "A hug and a serenade on demand?" she teased. "I'm gonna be spoiled by you."

His smile flicked wide, and she lost feeling in her right hip. "That's all right. I think you're worth it."

Kiss the man, Mandi's voice ordered in her head, taking her by surprise. *Kiss the man now!*

It wasn't a bad idea, either, but the distance posed a problem, as did the dog between them, and then there were the people around them . . .

And the fact that Brynn suddenly felt cold in her extremities while her heart exploded like a firework, the combination of which just made her feel dizzy.

No, she wouldn't kiss him. Not here, not now. Possibly not ever, if she were honest.

Full Rigged

But she'd hold his hand while they lay here beneath the stars.

And that was certainly something.

Chapter 13

Lost Creek Days was insane.

Probably fun to attend if you were local or had traditions, but when you were an outsider trying to help, the thing was absolutely nuts.

And Ford wasn't that much of a people person anyway.

Why was he here?

All he'd wanted was to do his bit with the other guys, and now he was sitting here in a dunk tank.

How had he been roped into sitting in a dunk tank? Ryan was the local. Why couldn't he be the cowboy dunked?

Thankfully, everybody in Lost Creek had a terrible arm, and it was a family carnival, which kept him from having to deal with annoying teenagers. But it also meant he couldn't walk around with Brynn like he'd wanted.

Or help with Josie, if he were to be more altruistic.

He couldn't help with any of the Broken Hearts ladies, which he had been planning on, and getting pulled to sit in a box in full rodeo clothes was not the kind of interruption he appreciated.

Full Rigged

Sitting here, hovering over water, watching everyone else participate in the fun of the evening, was not enjoyable.

At all.

"And here, you will see the ever elusive cowboy in a box," Reid's voice called out from somewhere nearby. "Suspended over water, which, you will see, provokes a similar reaction to cats over water. And if we stare long enough, the cowboy's hair might stand on end. Folks, please don't tap the glass, it will disturb him."

Reid suddenly appeared in front of Ford, the crowd of Broken Hearts ladies and the rest of the Original Six in tow. The guys all grinned the same stupid smile, knowing how Ford would hate his current position and situation.

It occurred to Ford that it would be an opportune time to make any of a handful of gestures toward Reid under such a circumstance, but as there were ladies present, he would resist.

He could glare and scowl, but he'd keep his hands where they sat.

"Keep laughing, Chuckles," Ford mused, letting himself smile darkly. "One of you is next."

That wiped the smile from Reid's face faster than anything else could have, and suddenly none of the guys seemed as interested in heckling him.

Funny how that worked.

Except for West.

"What I wouldn't give to have Silvia's brother down here right now," West said on a sigh, still smirking at Ford's vulnerable position.

"Or Talia's cousin," Ryan pointed out, though without the same smirk.

Ford looked between the two. "Just because neither of you could hit the broad side of a barn with a baseball doesn't mean we need Major League players down here. Move along—go get yourself some popcorn or corn dogs." He nodded to the guests hanging out beside them. "Ladies. Enjoy the evening. I hear the Ballistic Swing is a good time, and the Wrecking Ball will turn your stomach. I'll front any of you money to challenge the boys here to the mechanical bull."

"Oh, it's on!" Trish gushed, rubbing her hands together and looking over the guys.

"Count me in, too!" Sadie called eagerly. She and Trish gave each other a high five, making the others laugh.

Lars exhaled with playful dramatization, and waved them to follow. "Fine, we'll head in that direction. Unless someone wants to knock Ford in the water first."

All eyes shifted to him for a moment.

He kept his expression carefully blank.

"Nah," Julia finally said with a firm shake of her head. "He's too nice for that. Are we going to pass a concession stand or food truck before we get there? I could use something bad for me."

"We just had dinner!" Trish told her in surprise.

Julia only shrugged. "When in Rome, eat the junk."

Knowing what he did, Ford smiled at that, and glanced at Brynn. She was already looking at him, and her small smile dropped the floor out from his stomach. The fact that it didn't drop the physical floor out from beneath him and land him in the pool of water there was nothing less than miraculous.

Just in case he hadn't known where he stood after lying under the stars with Brynn and holding her hand most of the evening, he was convinced now that he was in this with both feet. He had significant personal interest of a distinctly romantic nature that meant he'd be more than a little biased in helping her through her therapy experience here.

That wasn't selfish, was it?

The group started moving away, and Brynn was slower than the rest to do so. She waved at him a little, and his heart lurched to the side of his chest to follow her.

Dang. He hadn't been this crazy over a girl in years. Maybe never.

This was all new territory, and he couldn't say he minded all that much. Apart from the fact that she'd likely never fully trust a man again, given what her ex had put her through. She might not have any interest in dating or relationships for a long time. Maybe not ever, depending on how her therapy with Kellie went and what she decided for herself.

He'd support her no matter what, but he'd also start wishing that wasn't the case.

She *had* held his hand last night.

The fact that he was even thinking about that made him feel like a pathetic thirteen-year-old. Maybe even a girl—he wasn't sure. He'd never thought about stuff like that when he was thirteen, but he knew his sisters had.

He needed to stop thinking. At all. Maybe he could head out to Pete's after this and get in some late-night steer wrestling. Focus on something else that didn't make him feel so off-kilter.

The trouble was that even seeing his dog made him think of Brynn now.

Not okay.

Did either of his sisters ever have this problem?

Did Darren? He was too afraid to ask Tucker. He was a bit of a lady's man, and Ford couldn't be sure if he'd have a better or worse opinion of his little brother after that conversation.

"Well, well, well . . . That's not something you see every day. Motor in a box."

Ford's eyes widened as he scanned the crowd of carnival goers, knowing that the only people who would call him Motor would be people from home.

And also knowing exactly who was calling him that now.

There was a break in the group in front of him, and there she was. Light denim jeans, loose T-shirt, long, sandy hair braided and slung over a shoulder, and an all-too familiar straw hat sitting on her head.

"Shayla Belle, what are you doing here?" Ford demanded, unable to help grinning at the sight of his little sister, even if she was looking smug.

"Came to check out Lost Creek, big brother." She eyed the dunk tank target, her eyes narrowing. "Hmm. Someone really ought to give this a whirl."

Ford swallowed, shaking his head. "Shay, don't you dare."

But she was already handing over a five-dollar bill for three balls.

She'd only need one.

It was a little known fact outside of Montana, but Shay Hopkins could have gone into professional softball after college. All-American, full-ride scholarship, and the only softball player in the school's history to have five no-hitters to her name.

He was toast.

Before he could even pretend to hang onto something, Shay wound up and released a pitch so fast and screeching that Ford was positive it broke the target when it hit. But as he was dropped into the tank of water the moment it did hit, it was tough to say what exactly it sounded like.

He pushed off the bottom and squinted as his face broke the surface. Wiping the water out of his eyes, he looked out at his sister, now happily hugging a green teddy bear in a cowboy hat.

Ford shook his head, muttering incoherently as he turned and hauled himself out of the tank, feeling twenty pounds heavier in soaking-wet clothes.

Full Rigged

He took the towel offered by the local carnival volunteer before heading down the stepladder and nodded at Tom Hauser, the head honcho of Lost Creek Rodeo events, who was lined up to sit in the tank next.

"Good luck, man," Ford said as he passed.

Tom clapped him on the back with a grin. "Glenda's delighted I'm doing this. Too many days around the livestock in a row. I'm shocked she didn't put something fresh-smelling in the water."

Ford sniffed himself, then shook his head. "Sorry, just Lost Creek water."

Tom chuckled and climbed up to face his fate.

Ford was about to do the same.

Rubbing at his wet hair with the towel, he walked over to where his sister stood, swaying in place with her teddy bear like a six-year-old, her dimples on full display as she grinned at him. Ford didn't smile back, but that was only because he had a payback plan.

He'd smile when it was over.

Shay's grin grew wary as he approached, then faded completely, eyes wide, when she realized he wasn't stopping. "No, no, no, no, no, Ford, you can't . . ." She backed up hastily, bumping into a trash can behind her.

"Oh, yes, I can," he assured her, smiling mischievously now. "And I will."

Trapped as she was, Shay didn't have a chance, and Ford swept her into a tight, clenching, dripping-wet hug, taking care to rub his hair against hers for effect.

"Guhhhhhh," Shay groaned, wincing dramatically. "I should have seen that coming."

"Mile away, kid." He pulled back, smiling for real now. "Hiya."

She scowled up at him. "Hey. You got a change of clothes, or are you dripping the rest of the night?"

"Yeah, there's some in my truck. Come on." He moved to put his arm around her shoulders, but she blocked his arm.

"Don't touch me," she warned with a smile. "Huh-uh."

Ford snorted softly. "You're already wet, kid."

"Not as wet as you, and I'd like to keep it that way." She sniffed and adjusted the strap of her shoulder bag. "I don't have a handy change of clothes, and I'm not about to waste this carnival digging through my suitcase."

He gave her a sidelong look. "How'd you know it was Carnival Night?"

Shay only shrugged. "I didn't. I wanted to be here for your rodeo stuff, and I know how locked in your head you get right before, so I wanted to make sure I could actually spend time with you before that happens."

"I was just home, Shay."

"Yeah, and you were head to head with Darren the whole time or trying to convince Mom that you don't hate everything and everyone around." She gave him a scolding look that held too much understanding.

Ford looked away, shaking his head and wrapping the towel around his neck. "I *don't* hate everything and everyone. I love you guys. I love the ranch. I just . . . I don't know."

"It's not yours anymore."

He nodded, exhaling in relief that she got it, and smiled at her. "Yeah. It'll always be home, but it's not my home, you know?"

"You're restless," Shay explained in her usual blunt way. "You're a rover. Maybe you're tired of roving?"

"Maybe." He nudged her with his shoulder. "You didn't have anything better to do in Montana?"

Shay sighed noisily. "I had a fight with Mom. Which is impressive, I know, since she doesn't fight."

Ford sobered at that. Their mom was a tough woman, but

she was also a gentle woman. She rarely raised her voice and always made it a point to resolve differences in the family quickly. But their mother also had an incredible ability to stick to any topic of question and conversation over a lengthy period of time. Worse than any dog with a bone he'd ever met.

He'd been answering her questions about settling down for the past ten years.

She still didn't like his answers.

"What was it about?" he asked Shay gently.

"Same as always," she told him. "What am I going to do with my degree, when am I going to have a plan, and why don't I just get back together with Heath?"

Ford grimaced, hissing slightly. "Sorry... Maybe you're just more like me, Shay. Trying to find where you fit."

"You wish," his sister shot back, grinning quickly. Then she cocked her head to one side. "Actually, you may be onto something. I know Mom means well, and I probably shouldn't have snapped, but I don't know what I'm going to do or what my plan is. Every time she suggests options, it feels like a boulder in a backpack I can't take off. I spent all of college focusing on softball; school was just the vehicle for playing softball. So now I'm an adult with a degree, but no direction. I just need to figure that out, and it can't be on her schedule."

"I bet Carly didn't help there."

Shay sputtered, making him laugh. "Carly yelled at me for yelling at Mom, and then Tucker yelled at me for making Carly yell, and then Darren yelled at Tucker for yelling at everyone..."

That sounded about right.

"And Dad?" Ford asked, afraid of the answer.

Shay smiled softly. "Daddy told me to come visit you and get away for a while. I brought some new stuff for you to ride in with Darren's new logo, per Dad's particular request, and he just asked me to apologize to Mom privately and ignore the others."

That was an improvement, no question.

"Dad approved Darren's logo?" Ford grinned, elation lighting up his chest. "So he might actually step aside in some ways so Darren can do more."

"Baby steps, but maybe." She gave him a suspicious look. "You still want to know about Heath, don't you? Because I'm not getting back together with him, no matter how much Mom wants to share grandkids with Kathy."

"Didn't even cross my mind," Ford assured his little sister. "Never liked the guy."

She nodded firmly before smiling again as they walked.

That was close.

They reached his truck and he opened the door, grabbing the plastic bag containing his change of clothes.

"Did you know you'd be in the dunk tank tonight?" Shay asked as he closed the door and locked the truck again.

"I knew it was an option," he told her, indicating a line of portable toilets nearby. "There's a few options the Six could get pulled into tonight that could make a change of clothes necessary, so we all brought a set. I'm hoping West gets set up with the pie-face booth later."

Shay crossed her fingers and looked up to the sky. "Please, let West get pie-faced . . ."

Ford laughed. "They're gonna love seeing you, kid. It's been a while."

"Well, none of them really come to the Montana rodeos, and I don't travel much." She lifted a shoulder. "Mom would love hosting them if they'd come."

That wasn't a bad idea, if he could convince the guys it was worth the road trip. And if things were turning Darren's way on the ranch, it might prove to be a good trip outside of the rodeo parts as they showed off.

Full Rigged

Definitely worth considering.

He stepped into one of the portable toilets to change quickly into a clean T-shirt and a fresh pair of jeans. Thankfully, he hadn't worn boots or his hat when he was dunked. He'd have been a lot less pleasant if he had.

Shay was typing away on her phone when he came out, but she looked up at him with a quick grin when he appeared. "Ready, Freddy? I'm starving."

"Then let's get you fed!" He laughed and tried to put his arm around her again, and this time she let him. "Where are you staying?"

"I'll get a room across the street at the cute little B&B," she assured him with a wave of her hand. "Local businesses can always use money, right?"

Ford frowned a little. "Yeah, but there's a rodeo this weekend, so they'll have plenty. Why not come stay at the Prospers'? Kellie has room at the homestead house, even with her guests."

Shay whacked his chest with a flick of her hand. "What is it with you volunteering other people? I swear, you'd sign me up to run a marathon if you didn't know I'd beat you up."

"I would not," he protested. "I know exactly how much you hate running."

She rolled her eyes. "I'm not going to ask Kellie to make room for me at her retreat, Ford. She's working. She doesn't need to play hostess, too."

Ford was about to reply when he caught sight of part of the ranch group, and he grinned. "Oh, yeah? Hey, Kellie!" he called.

She turned in surprise, then smiled and waved. "Oh my goodness, is that Shay? Hi!" She hurried over and gave Shay a huge hug, which would have endeared her to Ford for life if he hadn't already been a fan.

"Hi, Kellie,' Shay replied, sounding surprisingly shy.

Kellie glared at Ford. "Why didn't you tell me she was coming?"

"Didn't know," he replied without hesitation. "Can she stay at the ranch with you?"

"Ford!" Shay all but screeched.

"Obviously!" Kellie overrode, widening her eyes. "Where else would she stay?" She returned her attention to Shay. "How long are you in town?"

Shay hesitated now, wincing a bit. "I'm not really sure?"

Kellie nodded decisively. "Perfect. I'll have Ryan put you to work on the ranch, then. You can show the guys how to really get the job done."

"I'll pay you for the trouble," Shay assured her.

"Uh, no, you won't." Kellie shook her head. "You'll be working the ranch, so that takes care of room and board. If you decide you want a job, we'll talk new arrangements, but that's neither here nor there."

"A job?" Shay looked at Ford, bewildered.

He could only shrug with a grin.

Kellie was Kellie, and she was going to do whatever she wanted.

Ford looked behind Kellie and saw Brynn, who was watching the exchange with a small smile.

His left thigh tightened in response.

Josie and Julia were also with them, but it was Brynn who held his attention. She met his eyes, and her smile turned brighter.

"She's so cute!" she mouthed, pointing through Kellie to Shay.

He could have kissed her for that.

He could have kissed her for a lot of things, but liking his sister instantly was pretty huge.

"Shay," Ford said suddenly, clearing his throat. "These are some of Kellie's guests. Josie, Julia, and Brynn. Ladies, this is my little sister, Shay."

"Hi," Julia said with a wave. "Your brother's pretty great, you know."

Shay grinned and wrapped an arm around his waist. "He's all right."

Josie smiled at her, though she seemed a little skittish in their surroundings. "I love your belt."

Ford hadn't even noticed, and looked over. It looked like someone had braided white rope and flattened it into a belt. Was that cute?

"Thanks!" Shay said brightly, absently rubbing it a little. "I guess I'm staying at the house, so I'll show you where I got it later."

"Great!" Josie was beaming now, and Ford wanted to hug his sister for giving her that.

Brynn came around Kellie so Shay could see her better. "You are just the cutest thing," Brynn told her immediately. "Like ranch-girl chic meets girl-next-door equals magic."

"And you might be my new best friend," Shay told her with a laugh, releasing Ford to give Brynn a hug. "I've never felt cute in my life. I'm about five-eight, and I'm built like Ford..."

"Hey, cute does not equal petite," Brynn told her as she pulled back. "Strong women are all shapes and sizes, and everything about you just works."

"And Brynn's a doctor," Kellie told Shay, nodding in agreement. "So she knows."

"What do I always tell you?" Ford said with a quick nudge to his sister.

She looked up at him. "Shut up and wait my turn?"

Everyone laughed, and Ford rolled his eyes. "No, kid, the other thing."

"I'm not a cookie cutter," Shay recited with a wink.

Ford nodded with pride, dropping his arm around her shoulders again and pulling her close to kiss the top of her head.

She elbowed him in the stomach half-heartedly in response.

Brynn smiled at the pair of them. "We were just heading to find Julia a milkshake and something of a little more substance for the rest of us. You hungry?"

"Starved," Shay groaned without shame. "I'll eat anything."

"Great!" Brynn's eyes flicked to Ford, making his heart skip, and the group turned to keep walking.

"You like her," Shay said in a low voice between the closed teeth of her smile.

Ford stiffened. "What?"

"Brynn. You like her. Not a question."

He exhaled very slowly. "How could you tell?"

"Your voice went all soft when you said her name," she informed him, stepping away a little. "And then there was the mushiness of this." She gestured to his face. "All of this, complete mush when you looked at her." Shay quirked her brows. "And I'm staying at the house with her."

With a flick of her braid, Shay turned to follow the rest, skipping ahead to link arms with Josie.

Ford followed the group reluctantly, his stomach crawling with nerves about the possibilities ahead.

Chapter 14

"And here's your change. Thank you! Have a good evening!" Brynn smiled and waved at the couple heading away from the booth, then sat roughly in the chair and let her face completely relax.

"Good faking."

Brynn glanced at the woman sitting beside her, smiling a little, meaning it more. "I wasn't faking all of it. I want them to have a good evening, and I did appreciate them buying something. It's a bake sale. Every purchase is welcome, right?"

Mariah dropped her head back and laughed a warm, throaty laugh. "That's perfect. Oh, Brynn, I love it. I get it, trust me. We've been out here all day. You've got to be tired."

"I've only done the afternoon shift," Brynn told her. "I can help out tomorrow, too."

"Trying to avoid ranch duty?" Mariah quipped, pushing up from her seat and starting to pick up the area around them.

Brynn only shrugged. "Trying to get more of your berry streusel muffins, actually."

Mariah gave her a bemused look, then reached for a box

tucked behind a stack of pies. "You don't have to work tomorrow to get some. Here."

Gaping, Brynn took the box. "Honestly, if I had known those were back there, I'd have eaten them. I mean, I'd have put money in the till for them, but they would be gone."

"Why do you think I hide them?" Mariah grinned and nudged her head toward Main Street. "Get out of here, girlfriend. You'll want to get to Open Mic Night."

"Let me help you get cleaned up." Brynn set her box down and moved around the front of the table to the very few items left on the display.

Mariah wagged a finger in her direction. "Huh-uh. Put that down. I've already texted my husband, and he's coming over to help me take stuff back to the shop. You've done more than enough today. Go over to Roosters and get something. The music is usually pretty good, and I'm not just saying that because I'm a local."

Brynn looked at all of the things Mariah and her husband would need to get back to the bakery. "Are you sure you don't want some help?"

"I do want some help," Mariah shot back. "From my husband. You've done more than enough. Be sure to come by tomorrow even if you aren't working. I'm in the pie contest."

"You'll win," Brynn scoffed with a dismissive hand. "But I'll come to watch you get the trophy."

Mariah laughed once. "It's an engraved pie pan, but thank you. And there's no guarantee I'll win. Not when Shannon Caldwell is competing. Her lemon cream pie is killer."

Brynn narrowed her eyes. "And how is your lemon cream pie?"

Mariah's lips twitched. "Very popular."

There was nothing to do but give Mariah a gesture that her answer was completely obvious. "I'll see you win your

Full Rigged

engraved pie pan tomorrow. Good night, Mariah." Brynn picked up her box of muffins and hefted them in a playful motion.

"Good night, darlin'. Have a good time."

With a wave, Brynn left the booth and headed up the road. Roosters was the most popular bar in Lost Creek. She had found that out the first few days she'd been here. It was only fitting that that would be the place for Open Mic Night—part of the Lost Creek Days schedule. Being a bar, it wouldn't be open for full families, which was why they had a Family Game Night going on at the public library.

For everybody else, Open Mic Night was apparently a highlight. It had been the topic of conversations for everyone she'd heard today, and she hadn't really understood why until one of the local gals volunteering to help in Mariah's booth had explained.

Lost Creek had a band. A bunch of guys, and occasionally a girl or two, who were local legends for their skills in guitar, banjo, fiddle, piano, and any other instruments that screamed Western music. Completely country and bluegrass, sometimes with vocals and sometimes not. But they always had a set of songs prepared for Open Mic Night at Lost Creek Days, and no one wanted to miss it.

Having that on the docket apparently made the other volunteers for the evening attain a certain level of skill before being brave enough to perform.

That was one way to keep embarrassing amateur acts from wasting people's night.

But what about the ones who could have been star amateurs? What about the more insecure ones who had just as much talent, but couldn't quite see it for themselves?

It was something Brynn was excited to see for herself. That and she needed a drink.

Preferably something that would go well with her muffins.

Then again, eating those in full view of others might not go well for her.

She didn't have time to get back to the ranch before the others would be in town for Open Mic Night, so she'd have to find a way to stash them somehow.

Hide them.

The sound of a car door brought Brynn's attention out of her muffin-hiding plot, and she found herself grinning before she could help herself.

It had actually been a truck door that she'd heard.

Ford's, to be precise.

Shay was with him, which was ridiculously cute, and they both looked like perfect pieces of the Lost Creek scene, despite being temporary transplants in it. Ford was full cowboy in a western-cut button-up with a striking black, blue, and white plaid pattern and some clean but faded jeans that carved a perfect line up his thighs and hips.

How in the world had he done that while buying standard jeans? The man was the furthest thing from fashionable she'd seen, without being offensively so, and yet there wasn't a woman on the planet who would find fault with how he looked in jeans.

And then there were his boots.

Were those things ever truly clean?

His hat cast his eyes in shadow, but they would have been as bright a blue as the hints on his shirt, crinkling with the smile he was giving his sister.

Then he looked at Brynn, and the smile grew.

There went her kneecaps.

How did he do that to her?

"Hey!" he called out, lifting a hand to wave as he moved around the front of the truck. "Heading in?"

Fighting a strange fluttering in her chest and stomach, Brynn nodded. "Yeah. I just finished over at the bake sale." She wrinkled up her nose as she glanced down at her box of muffins. "Would it be okay if I stash these in your truck? I'm afraid if I take them in there, they'll be gone no matter where I hide them."

Ford eyed the box, still too far to really see inside. "Are those berry streusel muffins?"

"Might be," she said lightly, something ticklish shooting down one leg.

"Do I get one if I say yes?"

"Will you say yes for a maybe?"

Shay released a giggle that she bit back, watching the two of them like a tennis match.

Ford's smile softened, and Brynn lost her breath in an instant. "Absolutely."

"It's not locked yet," Shay told her in an undertone.

Brynn nodded and hurried over, opening the nearest door and sliding the box onto the seat. "Thanks," she told Shay, running a hand through her hair and tousling it.

"Not her truck," Ford pointed out, still grinning at the two of them.

Shay rolled her eyes and looped her arm through Brynn's. "Ignore him. You look great for working a bake sale booth all day."

"I feel sweaty," Brynn confessed as they moved toward the entrance of Roosters. "Thank goodness these off-shoulder tees are in right now, so I don't actually sweat through it."

"Perks, right?" Shay looked her over quickly. "Still. That jewel green is beautiful with your eyes and your hair. It just works."

Brynn blushed a little, seeing as how the girl was complimenting her appearance in front of the guy who . . .

Well, who made Brynn's stomach flip and butterflies rush inside her chest. That's who.

"Well, I may be underdressed, who knows?" she grumbled half-heartedly. She quickly turned her attention to Shay instead. "I love this ensemble. Reminds me of home. And your hair is fantastic all loose and curled."

Shay had gone with a western shirt as well, though hers had a distinctly Aztec vibe to it, with lots of turquoise hints, and she'd put on turquoise jewelry to match. Paired with a turquoise belt buckle and some dark-wash jeans, she would have any attention she wanted tonight, especially when her sandy-blonde hair hung around her shoulders like she was some cowgirl angel. If there was dancing in this place, she'd be dancing all night.

More than Brynn would be, at any rate.

"Where's home again?" Shay asked her.

"New Mexico. Recently home, anyway. And who knows what the future holds?"

As though her subconscious took over, Brynn glanced over at Ford with a hesitant smile. Her eyes fell to the guitar case he carried, and her smile pulled to an all-out grin.

"What?" he demanded, matching her smile as he held the door for them both. "What's that for?"

"Are you playing tonight?" she asked with a squeal, not bothering to hide how excited the thought made her.

Ford ducked his chin, glancing over at the street in a bashful way. "Might be."

"The Lost Creek Wranglers asked him to join them for the last two numbers of their set," Shay told her in a loud whisper. "Because he's amazing."

"That's fantastic!" Brynn gushed as she took his free hand, squeezing hard. "I can't wait to hear it!"

Ford looked at their hands before looking up at her,

making her shiver as he did so. "Just remember what I told you about my playing. Don't forget it, now."

That made her shiver, too.

"I won't," she assured him, sliding her hand from his with a slow fire that somehow traveled to her pinky toe.

He nodded and nudged his head toward the inside, then followed when she and Shay entered.

"What is it with people here using their heads to point?" Brynn whispered to Shay.

"It's a thing," came her soft reply. "And not just here. What did he tell you about his playing?"

Brynn clamped down on her lips hard and shook her head.

Shay scoffed loudly, looking away. "Girl, I will get you drunk and make you tell me."

"Fat chance," Brynn said with a laugh. "I hear you're pretty musical yourself, Shay Hopkins."

"Not like Ford," Shay insisted, shaking her head. "I can sing a little, but he doesn't even have to. What he can do with the guitar is extraordinary."

If she hadn't thought the siblings were related before, that would have cemented it. Neither of them would accept praise for themselves and had to lift up the other instead. It was adorable, and it was maddening.

And, apparently, it was the way the Hopkinses were.

"Whatever," Brynn told her, rolling her eyes. "I've seen the video on Eric's channel of you two. I know you both are fantastic."

"Nobody asked me to get up on stage with them tonight," Shay pointed out with a grin. "Now let's get some grub, I'm starving."

"You're always starving," Ford grumbled good naturedly behind them.

Brynn gave him a look over her shoulder. "I like a girl who isn't afraid to eat."

He raised a brow. "So do I."

There was no mistaking his point with how he looked at her.

Was he saying . . .? Did he mean . . .?

Emotions suddenly caught fire within her, and she thought for a moment that she was going to surge. But then her ears began to burn, and her fingers went numb, none of which ever happened in a surge, but definitely happened when she was embarrassed.

She could handle embarrassed.

But was it happy embarrassed? Or terrified embarrassed?

"The wings here are really good," Ford said, his smile curving in some private amusement she was afraid to think about. "And the ribs, when they're on the menu. Something really sexy about a woman who eats ribs."

Okay, that made her mouth go dry.

What in the world was getting into him?

What was getting into her?

"Good to know," she managed to say around her sudden cottonmouth. She shifted her attention to the tables and chairs in the place, arranged to accommodate the risers set up into a makeshift stage. There were booths lining the walls, and it seemed like the stage area was permanently arranged for something of the sort, though not on the same scale. Maybe for karaoke? And a part right in front of it was clearly arranged for dancing.

It was exactly the kind of bar Brynn liked, when she went to them. Open, comfortable, light, and full of local shoutouts. Pictures of rodeo events dotted the wall, as well as the occasional horseshoe, lasso, and even a few sets of spurs.

There weren't too many people in the place yet, and already Brynn loved it.

"Kellie asked us to grab a couple of tables near each other," Shay told Brynn, steering her toward one. "Think we can pull one or two over to this one?"

Brynn shrugged. "I don't see why not. Let's do it."

They set about arranging the area for the others who would come, though they wouldn't know how many of the guests at the ranch would show up until they actually did show up. All of the guys would come, they could say that for certain, but, as with all social opportunities for the guests, nothing was required or expected.

When the tables had been rearranged, Brynn sat in one of the bar stools, reaching into the bowl of peanuts sitting there. "I'm really excited for this," she told Shay with a bright smile. "A night out has been needed, especially one without the pressure of dating or anything."

"I hear ya," Shay agreed, nodding eagerly as she slid into a chair. "Although I think one of us is going to have a more interesting night than the other."

Brynn stared at her, wishing she didn't have any idea what Shay was saying. "Really?" she asked in a matter-of-fact tone, hoping the doubt in her voice would detract from Shay's suspicions.

Shay gave her a look that told her she wasn't fooled. "If you can't see it, I'm not saying."

Before Brynn could ask about that not-quite-cryptic statement, Ford came over to their table. "Alrighty," he began with a quick exhale. "I talked to Scottie at the bar. You both are on my tab tonight, no arguments. He's sending a menu over in a minute. Get whatever you want. I'm supposed to go get a quick rehearsal in with the band, and I'll see you when I can."

"That's really not necessary," Brynn protested.

He put a hand on her back, giving her a hard look, even

as he smiled that same stomach-flipping smile he always did. "What did I say about arguing?"

He looked across the table to his sister. "Rumor has it I may have a solo song later. Wanna sing it?"

Shay looked surprised, but nodded after a moment's hesitation. "Yeah. Got a preference?"

Ford shook his head. "Whatever you want. Might not even happen, but if it does, just let me know what you want to sing when you get up there." He nodded to them both, then turned and weaved around the tables toward the back of the place.

Brynn watched him go, something in her chest lurching after him.

Absolutely nuts.

A group of high schoolers got up on the risers with their guitars, one of them sitting at the drum set, and began playing some country version of house music, which was actually pretty good. Brynn wouldn't get up and dance to it, but she wasn't much of a dancer anyway. It could be danced to by those who did consider themselves dancers, but without a few drinks in her, that was not Brynn.

Even with a few drinks in her, that wasn't really Brynn.

Usually.

"Hi there," a chipper young woman of maybe twenty-two chimed near them. "I'm Stacey. Scottie says you guys might want some food, so I've brought some menus. Since we're in Lost Creek Days, everybody gets chips and salsa on the house, and since Ford's performing, I can offer y'all a free order of onion rings and fries." She placed the menus on the table, her blue-streaked brown hair bouncing wildly in its high ponytail. "Wanna start with some drinks?"

They quickly ordered drinks and looked over the menu, giggling like kids over the delicious options before them.

Others from the ranch started to trickle in when their drinks arrived, and soon they were all chatting while waiting for food.

Josie and Meredith had decided to stay behind at the ranch, not really feeling the evening's events, but the rest of them had come out, including Kellie. And they were ready for a night on the town.

"Oh man," Paige groaned when Brynn and Shay's food came out. "Why didn't I order something? That mac and cheese looks killer!"

Brynn gestured at it. "Have at it. I don't need this whole thing. And it's the best mac and cheese I've ever had in my entire life, so . . ."

Paige didn't need telling twice, and started in on it with a clean fork.

Julia shook her head, exhaling a short sigh of irritation. "I can't decide. I'm gonna go order an appetizer sampler. Anyone need something?"

"I got it," Lars told her, waving her down. "Reid and I will get drinks. Who wants what?"

They shouted out their orders, Julia pointedly asking for a Diet Coke, which drew some curious looks from Sadie and Trish, but they said nothing.

The microphone on the stage was tapped, drawing attention there.

"Good evening, Lost Creek!" a man in a black T-shirt and a neat beard said with some enthusiasm.

The bar cheered in response, a few people raising their glasses in salute.

"For those of you visiting us for this year's Lost Creek Days, my name is Scottie Henderson, and I'm the general manager of Roosters." He paused while the room erupted in applause again. "I'd like to thank the Ramblin' Ropers for getting us started, and doing a great job. Guys, we look forward to hearing what you can bring to us next year as headliners."

The teens grinned at that, giving each other high fives even as the crowd cheered their approval.

"We're gonna start off tonight's Open Mic Night with the guys and gals you've all been waiting for," Scottie told them all, grinning widely. "Ladies and gents, put your hands together for the Lost Creek Wranglers!"

Brynn and the others cheered as a group of western-clad men and women got up on the stage, a few of the guys sporting impressive beards. Ford wasn't among them, but Shay had said he would be playing only a few numbers in the set.

So where was he now?

"Don't worry about it," Shay told her as an upbeat song started. "He likes to get his head in the game, and this is definitely something he needs to be on his game for."

"But you don't?" Brynn asked with a smile.

"Nope!" Shay grinned and took her hand. "Come on, let's dance." She waved at the other guests, and soon they were all out on the dance floor together, laughing and dancing.

Brynn hadn't felt freedom like this in years. This release of inhibitions and breaking free of the burdens that had weighed down on her ever since the stories about her ex-husband had begun to come out. She was just Brynn Kershaw now, not the duped wife or the troubled doctor not the blind woman whose husband slept around or the poor lady whose marriage crumbled into dust.

Just Brynn.

She hadn't been her in a long, long time.

After a few songs, Brynn went back to the table for a break, gratefully accepting a glass of water from a waitress walking near the table.

"You look like you're having fun," Eric told her from where he sat watching everything.

"I am," Brynn told him with a grin. "Didn't think I would, but I am."

Eric nodded, his smile warm. "Good. You deserve it. You all do. I'd never thought much about what Kellie does back at the ranch, but lately . . . Wow, I think you ladies might be just as impressive as she is."

Touched, Brynn swallowed with some difficulty. "Thank you. I promise, we don't feel very impressive, but . . ." She laughed and reached over to squeeze his hand in gratitude. "It's very sweet of you to say so."

"I'm not that sweet," Eric assured her with a chuckle, patting her hand. "Just honest. Which I know you appreciate." He nudged his head toward the dancing. "I'm gonna go snag a dance with Shay before someone else does. She's like a kid sister, and I need to catch up."

Brynn nodded her approval and sat back in her chair, the moments of rest welcome.

"Ladies and gents, please welcome to the stage our friend and member of SHCC's Original Six, Ford Hopkins!"

Whistles and cheers sounded from all around, the bar fuller now than it was when the band had first started, and seeing Ford shyly get up on the stage, with only a slight wave for those cheers, was extraordinary.

A hot thrill of pride shot through Brynn from top to bottom as she watched him play. He was even better than she had seen in the video clip, keeping up with all of the seasoned players without any trouble and occasionally having moments where he just shone through the others. He was as unpretentious on stage as he was off it, wearing the same small smile that she adored. He loved being up there, she could tell, and he didn't care about any of the attention.

Maybe that was why there were no recent videos of him playing, even though he clearly had been doing so.

He didn't do it for attention.

He did it for love.

And that was Ford, she decided.

Everything he did was all in, all heart, all for the love of it, and he didn't care if anybody noticed or saw, or if it gained him any attention. He just wanted to do whatever it was he cared about.

So what did that mean as far as Brynn was concerned?

"Woo!" The lead singer for the Lost Creek Wranglers stepped up to the mic after their final song, wiping his brow and grinning at them all. "We'd like to thank y'all for hanging in there with us while we plunked out a few of our favorites. We're done for the night, but we got a real nice treat for you. Our buddy and adopted bandmate Ford is gonna spin you a song without us playing backup. Then I think when he's done, the mic really is open to whoever else. Have a great night, y'all. I'm gonna get me a beer." He flashed a double thumbs-up before exiting the stage with his bandmates, leaving only Ford up there.

Ford stood up and went to the mic, his guitar almost cradled in front of him. "Evening, y'all," he rumbled with a crooked smile.

The rest of the Original Six whooped embarrassingly loud, and several of the Broken Hearts ladies joined in, not that the crowd needed their additions.

The applause made Ford chuckle softly, which made Brynn smile. "I know Rick said I was going to spin you a song, and I promise to do that, but I'd rather not do it alone. So, if it's all right by you, I'm gonna ask my baby sister, Shay, to join me up here. She sings way more pretty than I do."

Cheers sounded while Shay made her up to the stage, and Brynn clapped for them both, feeling a burst of nerves on their behalf that she hadn't expected.

The siblings conversed quietly while Ford covered the mic, and then he nodded, patted his sister's back, and stepped back just enough to make sure she had center stage.

Because he was Ford.

"This song goes out to my new friends at the Broken Hearts Ranch," Shay said with a smile, staring right at the group of them, her eyes drifting to Brynn as well. "You have no idea how much I look up to you already. Love you ladies." Her smile spread, and Brynn thought she detected a hint of tears in her eyes, but Shay looked at her brother then, and it was impossible to tell for sure.

Ford began to play a slower song than they'd heard yet that night, and the absence of other instruments focused everyone's attention there. Every now and then, his fingers would tap against the wood of the guitar for a hint of percussion, and the combination was almost hypnotic for Brynn.

Then Shay began to sing, and it was almost the same voice Brynn had heard in their video, but now it had matured into something that reached directly into her chest and pulled at her heart. Something soulful and natural, an instrument all its own and without any equal.

It paired perfectly with Ford's playing, and Brynn was captivated by them both.

The song was a ballad that mixed blues with bluegrass and country, and spoke of inspiration and courage, of finding strength and comfort in each other, of never being alone, and of supporting each other through hard times.

It was a love song for human beings, and when Brynn considered Shay's dedication to them, there was nothing to do but cry.

A hand on Brynn's shoulder caused her to turn, wiping at her tears.

Ryan stood there, smiling with understanding. "I think you need to dance to this song, Brynn. May I?"

"I'm not really in a dancing mood," she apologized through her tears. "And besides . . ."

"Hey," Ryan interrupted very gently, stooping to meet her eyes directly. "I'm happily in a relationship, and Ford can't dance with you right now. But I promise he would if he could, so I'm just gonna stand in so you don't have to be alone for this song. This is special, Brynn. Come on."

Well, when he put it like that . . .

She nodded, swallowing a lump in her throat, and took his hand, letting him lead her out to the dance floor, where others were slowly dancing in pairs—not quite a romantic setting, but one of connection and feeling.

Ryan pulled her close, his hand settling safely at her back with one hand in hers, swaying gently. He winked at her, nudging his head toward the stage.

She looked, only to find Ford smiling at her as though they really were dancing together. No irritation with Ryan for taking his place, no indication that he saw anything other than her. Just her.

Just Brynn.

Her tears began to well up again, and she found herself resting her cheek against Ryan's shoulder while she stared at Ford as he played.

He never looked anywhere else. Not even at Shay, who was spinning the most beautiful moment for them with her song.

They might have been alone in a room with a song playing on the radio and dancing slowly together.

She hadn't felt so connected or so exposed in so long, and she felt such peace with it. No anger, no panic, no nerves at the overwhelming emotions she was feeling.

She just felt them. More than that, he was feeling them with her.

She wasn't alone.

She managed to smile at him through her tears, held securely in Ryan's arms so she could be connected to someone physically while she connected to Ford from a distance. While she let herself go, feeling safe enough to do so.

Ford's smile grew as he watched her, something impossibly sweet and tender in it.

Brynn sighed against her stand-in for the remarkable man playing for her and her alone right now.

She was falling hard for Ford Hopkins, there was no doubt about that.

No doubt at all.

CHAPTER 15

SOMETHING HAD CHANGED DURING Ford's song with Shay. The earth had shifted beneath his feet or the wind suddenly came out of the west or some magic spell had been cast. Something.

Because he had never seen Brynn Kershaw give him a look like that, and despite never kissing her, never telling her how he felt, never taking her on a date, he had become hers.

It was as simple and profound as that.

Terrifying and confusing, definitely didn't make sense, but that's where he stood.

If he'd had a little less restraint, he'd have escorted her out to the back of the bar and kissed her until dawn just for the connection they'd felt in the song.

But he hadn't, and he wouldn't.

He knew she had felt something during the song, and certainly that she felt something for him, there was no denying that. But he could not, would not, push her in any direction or in any way to admit to whatever he thought those feelings should be. She had been through enough in her life with being told what somebody else wanted her to believe. She deserved the space and the freedom and the respect to act as she saw fit, when she saw fit.

No matter how it might affect him.

He hadn't done much after his song, mostly because he was no dancer. He could slow dance easily enough, but what in the world did you do for the rest of the songs? Jump up and down like a pogo stick?

There were always the line dances, but those didn't hold much interest either. He'd much rather play the songs than participate in them.

Brynn had been quiet, so he hadn't pressed anything there. Shay had been having a great night, in her element, dancing and hanging out with the other ladies, and enjoying catching up with the Six. The guests seemed to be enjoying themselves, which was always worth seeing, and he made sure to keep an eye on anyone approaching them. Things were generally okay with the locals; they respected Kellie enough to respect her guests. But with rodeo events coming up at the end of the week, people from out of town would be coming in, and those people didn't know the boundaries.

At a place like a bar, they were more at risk with those people.

Most of the ladies could hold their own and wouldn't need anybody's help to get out of a situation like that. But every now and then, they'd get someone like Josie, and he'd go ten rounds in a boxing ring to get someone to stay away from her.

And that was just Ford. The others would do the same, which would pose a pretty interesting threat for whoever was trying to make a play for a woman they had no business even approaching.

Julia had come over to him at one point and asked if he'd

mind driving her back to the ranch. She was exhausted, and not feeling great, and given what he knew about her condition, he'd immediately agreed to take her back so she could rest, if not go to bed. Brynn had seen the look of concern on his face and appeared beside them, clearly on a doctor's high alert, and insisted on accompanying them back to the ranch.

So even if he'd wanted to spend part of his evening with her, that effectively put an end to it.

But he didn't mind all that much. The best thing for all of them was that the guests were well and safe, if not comfortable. And Brynn might be a doctor when it came to Julia, but she was a guest, too, and she would need to make sure she was taking care of herself as well.

He wasn't going anywhere.

So here he sat on the couch in the cabin he and Eric had settled in—the other bedroom going to Reid now that he was in town—yawning as he prepared for bed. Everybody had come back in the last hour or so, and Eric and Reid had headed straight for their designated bedrooms. Why exactly Ford wasn't working on actual sleep like they undoubtedly were wasn't too much of a surprise to him.

Rodeo was coming up.

He'd need to do some decent practice rounds in the next few days with the rodeo events starting on Friday. The others would feel the same way, and with Ryan's ranch running full go with all of the employees now on site, there was less pressure on them to help out with the work.

It really was perfect timing, all things considered.

The only question he really had was if he could convince Ryan to take time away from the ranch to train with him.

His phone buzzed suddenly and he blinked, pulling it from the table near the couch where he'd set it down.

A call was coming in, and it was from Brynn.

At this time of night?

He hit the answer button and brought the phone to his ear. "Brynn?"

"Hi," she said on an exhale he didn't like at all. "Um . . . You answered, so are you up?"

"Yeah . . ." he said slowly, sitting forward and frowning. "What's wrong?"

"Can you come out? I need to talk."

Ford shot to his feet, looking out the window. "Brynn, are you here?"

"Almost," she admitted with a little laugh he didn't trust. "I need to talk, and I only wanted to talk with you."

"Okay." He nodded, questions spiraling in his mind but not changing his decision. "Okay, yeah, I'm coming out." He grabbed his jeans and tugged them on, fumbling for a T-shirt, too.

"Great, thanks."

Brynn hung up before he could ask or say anything else, giving him time to get his clothing completely on and straightened. He shoved his phone into the back pocket of his jeans and headed for the door, his heart pounding as he tugged on his boots that were sitting there.

What had happened? Why was she walking out on the ranch this late at night? Had he said something or done something to upset her? Had someone else?

Why wasn't she talking to Kellie, who was in the same house as her?

He stepped out of the cabin, closing the door softly, and walked out onto the gravel, no other sound in the night but that crunching beneath his feet.

There was something oddly ominous about that, and his pulse echoed the feeling in his ears.

He slid his hands into his pockets, turning a little in the road, not sure which direction she would be coming from.

Then suddenly, she was there, wrapped in a long sweater, her arms tightly folded, walking quickly toward him, her eyes down. She was determined in whatever she was thinking, and he didn't see any signs of the anxiety he'd noticed that day when he'd watched her surge in the pasture. Didn't mean she wasn't headed in that direction, he knew, but he didn't feel quite so worried about that scenario.

She looked up when she got closer, and her quick smile settled his stomach, weak though it was. "Hey."

"Hey," he replied softly, looking her over. "You okay?"

She started to nod, then changed her mind and shook her head. "No. Not really. I mean, I'm happy to not be out of my head with rage right now, but I'm not sure this feels much better."

"Need a hug?" he offered at once. He opened his arms in suggestion.

Brynn smiled again, and this one had tears to it. "I will, but let me see if I can get this out first."

Ford nodded, hooking his thumbs into the pockets of his jeans.

She exhaled slowly, her knees locking and unlocking in alternating patterns. "I got an email from my ex. He's not supposed to contact me directly; I have a 'Do Not Contact' order against him from when he wouldn't stop harassing me in divorce proceedings. He's only supposed to contact my lawyer. But he emailed my hospital account, so it got through to me, and . . ."

A snarl of hatred and disgust began to curl in Ford's chest and stomach, but he said nothing and waited for her to go on.

Brynn snorted in derision. "He wants me to testify on his behalf as a character witness in a sexual harassment case against him. Since he always treated me well, he says, I could show the courts that he's not the scum they're making him out to be. Despite the fact that he *is* the scum they're making him out to be, and now that he doesn't have a wife, he's free to sleep wherever and with whomever he likes without any stigma attached. Those are my words, not his. He says he's completely innocent."

Unbelievable, it was on the tip of Ford's tongue to say, but, again, he wouldn't say anything while she had more to share.

"I just . . ." She shook her head, swallowing hard. "I can't believe he actually thinks I have any desire to help him. That he doesn't see what he has done to me. That somehow my view of him would be an improvement on what any of these women accusing him see. I have no idea how many, but there's gotta be more than one if I know Trent. He's never been a guy who likes one-hit wonders. And that's his wording, not mine. From the divorce proceedings. When he was actually admitting stuff to me." She choked out a half-sob and looked up at the night sky. "Why can't he just disappear from my life?"

Ford opened his arms and took two steps forward. "Come here."

She scurried over and wrapped her arms around his waist, her hold clenching as she exhaled another sob against him. He wrapped his arms around her, cradling her into his chest and holding her as tightly as he dared, even as his heart raced with his own anger.

How dare this guy weasel his way into Brynn's life again, especially to ask for a favor so incomprehensible. What possessed him to think she somehow owed him anything at all? He'd taken enough from her over the years, and now that she was trying to find a better direction for herself, he wanted more?

"I hate him," Brynn whispered, shaking in Ford's arms.

"I hate that he still affects me in any way, and I hate that I actually thought about it for half a second. I hate the version of myself he brings out."

Ford brought a hand up to curl his fingers into her hair. "Don't say that," he whispered, pressing his lips to the top of her head. "Don't."

"But that's how I feel," she admitted in a raw tone. She turned her face to rest her cheek against his throat. "How can he still make me feel guilty for saying no? What is wrong with me?"

"Nothing," Ford insisted as his fingers rubbed against her scalp in what he hoped was a soothing manner. "You have a good heart, and you loved him once. That's hard to get rid of completely, no matter what you've been through."

Brynn nodded, hugging herself closer to him in a way that broke his heart. "I've been taking down my walls here, training myself to be okay with hurting and being vulnerable. It's hard and it's terrifying, but it's also liberating. I didn't think he could get to me here. And now I feel like that woman who sat on her couch and tried not to dissolve into thin air as her husband confessed to affair after affair as though it were a sporting event. I promised myself she'd never come back, but here she is." She sniffled softly, one hand releasing him to swipe at her face before returning to its place around him.

Ford couldn't say anything. He just pressed his lips to her hair and left them there, breathing in the scent of her and praying that somehow, this connection could give her healing.

"I'm not going to dissolve here, though," Brynn said with a wavering strength in her voice. "Not here. I'm firmly on the ground, and he doesn't get to expect anything from me, no matter what he threatens."

"What did he threaten?" Ford asked cautiously, his mouth still at her hair.

Brynn exhaled in irritation. "He said he was nicer than he should have been in the divorce settlement because he felt bad for cheating. Which is a lie—he's never considered it cheating since he was never faithful to me in the first place. He says he can get his lawyer to renegotiate terms and take more from me. Which is rich, since my lawyer ran circles around his and won't give him anything. And I'll be damned if I give him an inch."

"That's my girl," Ford praised, smiling against her and hugging her tight.

"He won't break me," Brynn vowed. "I bent over backwards to make my marriage work and spent years thinking I was to blame for the distance I could feel between us. Turns out I was being twisted and manipulated into a nervous wreck by a compulsive liar who never actually wanted to give me anything in life. I was a convenient cover for the lifestyle he wanted to live. My salary allowed him to do whatever he wanted. He loved flying, he said, and didn't want to give it up yet. No, what he loved was regular trips away from me to give him excuses and opportunities."

How anyone could want to be away from Brynn was unfathomable, and how anyone could even consider cheating on her . . .

Well, Ford was still seething about that one.

"I had to talk to you," Brynn admitted in an almost whisper. "As soon as I read the email, as soon as I hurt, I wanted to come see you. I needed to be safe."

"I'm here," he murmured, finding words more difficult with that admission. "I'm right here. You're safe with me, darlin'. Always will be."

She sighed and seemed to soften into him more. "I know."

If he weren't raging with anger, if she weren't recovering from being upset, he'd have kissed her for that.

His list of would-have kisses was growing a little long for his taste.

"I'll tell Kellie, too," Brynn assured him, as though his pause had been a question or suggestion. "She'll want to talk this out, or at least hear my thoughts. And I sent the email to my lawyer. So it's all done. It's just . . ." She sighed again. "It's confusing. And you make things less confusing, and calmer, so here I am."

He managed a smile she wouldn't see. "Glad I could help. So you're better now?"

"Better, yeah." Brynn stirred in his hold. "I can walk back now."

He didn't budge. "Not yet. See, you're calm, which is fantastic. But I'm gonna need a minute more, since I still want to rip your ex apart limb by limb and feed him to coyotes."

Brynn coughed a laugh and linked her hands together behind him, now seeming to be holding him more than he was her. "Okay, then. That's really sweet, in a slightly disturbing way, so I'll just hold you until it passes."

"Might be here all night, then," he grunted, resting his chin on her head. "I'm gonna be mad for a long time."

"I know a little something about that." She surprised him by turning her face and kissing his chest directly over his heart. "You have a good heart, too, Boy Scout. The absolute best."

How he managed to not emit the guttural sound his mind was making was an absolute miracle, as was the fact that he could stand upright when his kneecaps had clearly fallen to his toes.

"Well," he all but squeaked, "it's going a little crazy right now, if you can't tell. But thanks."

She giggled a low sound that reverberated through him. "You're very welcome." She lifted her face to smile up at him. "I think I left my muffins in your truck. Can we go get them?"

He grinned down at her, anger at her ex fading into delirium that he was with her. "I was holding them hostage. Got a negotiator?"

Her eyes narrowed. "What were you going to demand in exchange?"

As he didn't feel it was appropriate to admit his first choice of requests, he opted for the next one. "A walk with you," he said simply. "Where I get to hold your hand."

"We've already done that," she reminded him.

He shook his head slowly. "I want to really hold your hand, not hold your hand just to support you."

Her eyes widened. "Oh." Then her smile returned, an adorably shy edge to it. "You can hold my hand while we walk to the truck. And I already said you could have a muffin."

"You said maybe," he reminded her. "It wasn't a sure thing."

Brynn's eyes fell to his mouth, and his heart stopped. "It is now."

Before his heart could start again, Brynn went up on her toes and touched her lips to his, the action tentative and sweeter than any honey he could have tasted. He cupped her cheek with one hand and returned the kiss gently, careful to let her lead and follow her signals, no matter how his pulse thudded along his arms.

Her fingers dug into his back as she tried to arch further into the kiss, setting fire to him, but he resisted the madness she reached for. They needed to be slow and sure if they went there, even if their emotions went haywire.

He stroked his thumb along her cheek, layering kiss after kiss along her lips, content to continue at this pace if she was. She sighed against his mouth, making his hold on her tighten in response. She whimpered a laugh at that, her hands now trailing up and down his back in a way that was going to unravel him if it kept up.

How did one stop kissing a woman like this when it was so heavenly an experience?

Brynn broke off very slowly, her breathing unsteady and full of laughter, which made him kiss her again, and her hum of approval earned her one further still.

This was going to become a problem.

"Wow," she breathed when he managed to actually stop. "That should have been your demand."

Ford laughed and pressed a soft kiss to her brow. "It was going to be, but I wasn't sure I could say it."

Brynn gave him a dreamy smile he could have drowned in. "Next time, say it. I'm a fan."

He was going to kiss her again, and it was going to start the whole problem over. So he stepped back one step and took her now free hands, raising them to his lips and lingering there.

"Ugh," Brynn moaned. "You do know the way to a woman's heart."

He gave her a crooked grin. "I thought that was the muffins in the truck."

She considered that. "You may be right. Carbs."

"Thought so." He linked his hand with hers, lacing their fingers together, and started toward his truck with her, his kneecaps finding their way back to their preferred position as he did so.

His truck was parked next to the others, Westin's a ways away from them as per usual. It was an interesting line of pickups, that was for sure.

"Anybody would think you guys liked trucks," Brynn mused as they reached his.

"Functionality meets class," he said with a light shrug. "You're not gonna get very far on the ranch driving a Prius."

"Good point. Guess I hadn't thought about that." She smiled up at him, leaning against his truck. "I kinda want to drive one of the ATVs while I'm here. I've never done that. Ridden them, but never driven myself. Would that make me more of a ranch girl?"

He chuckled and rubbed his thumb over her hand, standing close. "Maybe. Not as much as riding a horse, though. Not all ranches have ATVs."

"Does yours?" she asked, cocking her head adorably. "Back in Montana?"

"Not yet," he told her. "My brother Darren wants to get a couple, but my dad is old school. The family ranch will stay pretty traditional until he gives it up."

Brynn reached up to touch his face, her fingers dusting across his cheek. "You sound so distant when you say that. Why?"

He shrugged, wanting to look away but powerless to do so when she stood in front of him. "It's not home anymore. It'll always be the family home, but it's not mine. I gotta find my place one of these days, a piece of land I can work and turn into my own. Somewhere to go and rest my hat when I can't ride in the rodeo anymore. I don't know where it is."

Her fingers cradled his jaw as she smiled at him. "You'll find it. There's no rush, right?"

No, there wasn't. And standing here with her like this, he really didn't find the need to rush anything at all.

He laughed very softly. "You're trying to make me give up that muffin you offered by being especially cute and taking my side, aren't you?"

She grinned, her eyes dark and luminous in the night. "Is it working?"

He leaned down to kiss her just once, very softly. "Nope," he whispered, reaching over to pull the door open.

She laughed and took the box he handed her, opening it with a dramatic sigh. "Fine, take your muffin, Boy Scout."

He plucked one out of the box without looking. "I think

we'd better get you back to the house. Kellie might have a curfew."

"I can walk," she assured him. "It's just over there."

"It's longer than you think," he pointed out. "I know, I've walked it."

She only smiled. "I'll need the alone time to overthink what just happened. Trust me, I'll be fine."

"I don't like you walking alone at night over there." He whistled sharply, and a clatter of paws sounded from the bed of the truck as Sherlock bounded down and came over to them. "Take this lug with you. He'll scare off snakes or whatever."

"Nice," Brynn said slowly, eying the ground she'd be walking. "Thanks for that image." Then she smiled down at the dog. "Why was he in the back of the truck?"

Ford smiled at Sherlock before looking back at Brynn. "Sometimes he prefers the truck outside to the warm comfort inside. Must be a ranch dog."

"Must be." She searched his eyes for a moment, then exhaled softly. "Good night, Ford."

He brought the hand he still held to his lips and kissed the back of it. "Good night, Brynn."

Her hand slid from his as she winked and started off in the direction of the homestead house, Sherlock trotting obediently by her side.

Ford watched her go for a minute, then started the walk back to his house.

"That was precious," Westin's voice said from beneath his truck as Ford passed. "How long has that been brewing?"

"Shut up, West," Ford snapped without malice. "Don't you have a racoon to cuddle with?"

Westin burst out laughing, and Ford kept walking toward his cabin, smiling to himself.

Not a bad day, all things considered. Not a bad day at all.

CHAPTER 16

IT WAS ONE OF the more emotional group sessions Brynn had attended yet, and she didn't actually mind that. It was Sadie's last day, and she was sharing her "So What" insights, as Kellie called them. Her thoughts on moving forward after the time she'd spent at the ranch. There was something so inspirational about hearing Sadie speak about her journey and how far she had come.

Of course, the ones who had been there longest were more emotional about her departure, but the ones who had only known her recently were also feeling the loss.

"So," Sadie said with a sniff, her tears clogging the word, "that's where I'm heading. Not gonna pretend it's gonna be a smooth ride, but I think I can handle it now. And that's the point, isn't it?"

Kellie nodded in approval, her smile fond for her guest. "That is the point. Absolutely." She looked around at the group, sighing heavily. "Well, does anybody else want to share something they've learned about their journey this week?"

Brynn twisted her lips, then raised her hand. "Yeah."

Kellie didn't seem surprised and gave her an encouraging dip of her chin. "Go ahead, Brynn."

"I learned that my angry surges," she began slowly, "are my defense mechanism against hurt. And because anger only spirals, it started to take over any big emotion. Stress, anxiety, nervousness, embarrassment . . . everything defaulted to anger, and because I was so torn up, I didn't have the ability to control it. My anger controlled me, and there was so much of it. When Trent finally told me about his cheating, and I saw him for what he really was, I was hurt and I was angry. Anger made me feel stronger than hurt, so I kept that. Not intentionally, but that's what happened."

Heads began to nod around the room, giving her comfort and sanity in this moment of admitting something she wouldn't have been able to before she got here.

Brynn smiled, tears beginning to form. "It's okay to be hurt. It's okay to be vulnerable. It's okay to be open. It's okay to not be protected by walls all the time. That's what I'm learning. I'm still learning how to be those things, but I haven't surged in forty-eight hours, and considering I'm dealing with therapy that leaves me drained and exposed, that's kind of miraculous."

"Not a miracle," Kellie told her, grinning at her like a mother, a sister, or a best friend. "That's you. That's your hard work and willingness to be open to change."

"It's still not comfortable to be vulnerable," Brynn said with a laugh.

"That's not going anywhere," Sadie quipped, crossing one leg over the other as she winked at Brynn. "Gotta get comfortable with uncomfortable."

Brynn made a face to show her feelings on that subject, which made the others laugh, too.

"Excellent sharing," Kellie praised. "Anyone else?"

"Me," Julia said quickly, shifting in her seat. "Umm . . . I've debated saying anything, but I decided it's part of my journey, and I need to share. I, um . . . I'm pregnant."

A gasp went up around the group, and Brynn smiled at her friend, suspecting what she was about to tell them all would be hard.

"When my mom passed," Julia went on, "it crossed my mind that she'd never see any kids I might have. Never meet my babies. I knew that, but since I didn't have any, it didn't feel real. But now . . . Alex and I are so happy, so happy that we're having a baby. We've laughed and we've cried, and then I sat in my room and cried some more. Because I can't call my mom and tell her that I'm going to have a baby." She broke down in tears and curled into a ball, sobbing the pain of her situation in front of them all.

Trish was sitting next to Julia, and wrapped her arms around her tightly, pulling Julia to lean against her as she cried.

"I want my mommy," Julia cried as the tears streamed down her face. "I'm having a baby, and I want my mom here for that. I don't know how to do this. I need her." She sniffed a little, clearing her throat. "I told Kellie that I feel like I've fallen back to where I was when I got here, and that I've lost all of my progress because this hurts more than I can handle." She covered her face with one hand, slumping against Trish.

"And what did I tell you, Julia?" Kellie prodded gently, handing Trish a box of tissues for her.

Julia lowered her hand to her mouth, swallowing hard. "It's okay that it hurts. Because I loved my mom, and losing someone you love should hurt. It's part of loving them. And that I just need to not get stuck in my grief."

Kellie smiled, wiping a tear away from her own cheek. "Exactly. You can be happy about the baby while being sad for your mom. That's okay, too."

Meredith sniffed back tears and pushed up from her chair, coming over to crouch before Julia, taking her hand. "Julia, I'm going to ask you a question. And I need you to really consider it, baby. Can you do that?"

Julia nodded, looking at her as she held onto Trish for support.

"I want to be your stand-in mama," Meredith told her. She smiled even as tears rolled down her cheeks. "I can't bring your true mama back, but I can give you a mama to call when you are scared, when you are hurt, when you need someone to cry with you, when your baby is coming and you just want her. I want you to call me. I'll come stay with you when the baby comes, talk to your mother-in-law about what you need, whatever you want. I'm here, okay?"

Well, there wasn't a dry eye among them after that, especially when Julia reached out and hugged Meredith tightly, both of them crying hard.

"Okay," Kellie said through her tears. "I think we're done. Let's give these two some time."

Brynn and the others left, some going back to their rooms to cry or journal or both, some going out to do chores or just breathe in the Texas air. Brynn was in that latter group, eager to try out the ATVs like she'd told Ford the other night, or maybe learn to ride one of the horses. Her chore of the day wasn't supposed to start until later, so she had time to kill.

Of course, what she really wanted to do was find Ford, but something held her back from doing so. It had been less than forty-eight hours since she'd kissed him the first time, and she had lost count of the number of kisses they'd shared since then. They didn't talk about what any of it meant, where any of it would go, and honestly, Brynn wasn't sure she cared yet. She didn't want to think too much about it, or she might start to panic.

She never wanted to panic with Ford. Ever.

Which was why she couldn't think about how she felt about him, or what she was doing with him. She didn't know, couldn't have said even to herself. She was just . . . being. Doing what felt good and right in the moment without worrying about tomorrow or any days after that. She couldn't plan for the future for herself, let alone involve someone else in it. The future was how she'd gotten into this mess in the first place.

A future with Trent. That's what she'd wanted, and she'd been the one to push him for that. He'd proposed to her after they'd had that conversation. In reflection as the divorce went on, the reality had come crashing down on Brynn that Trent had never once said he wanted a future with her. She'd told him, and that had apparently been enough for him to buy a ring.

She'd misread everything in their relationship. Every excuse he'd made, every concern he'd dismissed, every present he bought her to make up for something. Everything he'd done had simply been to keep her in the dark and keep her happy enough to shut up.

How could she trust herself after that?

Maybe that's what she should have shared in group session today. That her biggest fear now was that she had done this to herself. Trent was the villain—she wouldn't dispute that. But had she wanted their relationship so much that she had willed it into existence? If he had never wanted it, how could he be to blame for its dissolution?

Was she the problem?

There was something fundamentally wrong with that thinking, and she knew it. What she didn't know was where the truth of the matter actually lay. And how to get herself out of the cycle of destructive thinking that was now taking over more than her anger had.

Maybe she was more messed up than she'd ever thought. And Ford shouldn't have to deal with that.

If they weren't a thing, if there were no plans, then she could just enjoy it. Enjoy him. And he wouldn't have to know the rest of her mess.

Was that too much to ask?

"Hey, Brynn."

She looked up to see that she had walked to the barn without really paying attention, and now Ryan stood there at the entrance with his horse, giving her a bemused look.

How long had he watched her while she'd been lost in her thoughts?

"Hey," she said simply, forcing a smile.

He waited for her to say something, then laughed. "Need something?"

"I don't know," she replied, surprising herself with her honesty. "I'm supposed to help with the new stock horses when they come this afternoon, but I don't know what that means. And I don't know what I'm supposed to do in the meantime."

Ryan smiled at her rambling, which was comforting in a way. Maybe she wasn't the first guest to be confused about what she should do with a little extra time.

"Did my sister give you any assignments?" he asked as he started cinching buckles and such on the horse's equipment. "Trust me, I know better than to put ranch work above the real purpose here."

There was something adorable about the way he'd said that, and it made Brynn wish she was closer with her brothers. "No," she told him as she laughed. "Someone had a bit of a breakdown in group session, so she just suggested we leave and give them space."

Even that didn't seem to take Ryan by surprise. "Fair

enough. Well, do you want to do some sightseeing on the ranch? You can check out one of the ATVs if you want. Or you can help me and my cousin Holt with those new horses. Which are actually here already, we just haven't started prepping them for tomorrow's auction."

"I won't be in your way?" Brynn indicated the barn and the pen behind him. "I don't know a thing about horses, you know."

"Most of the guests who come here don't know a thing about horses," Ryan assured her. "Trust me, we're used to dealing with that. If you want to do it, I'd be happy to have you."

Brynn considered that, then nodded. "I'd probably get lost trying to take the ATV out. Horrible sense of direction without landmarks."

Ryan chuckled. "We have landmarks."

"Right," she retorted, gesturing to the land around them. "Turn left at the anthill?"

"No, you turn right at the anthill," he shot back. "It's the snake hole where you turn left."

Brynn shuddered, making a face. "What is it with you guys and the snakes? Nobody wants to know about that."

"Perks of the ranch, darlin'." Ryan grinned and waved her over. "Come on, we'll give you a quick intro."

It didn't take long for Ryan to make her comfortable around all of the horses, considering all she was really going to do was lead the horses around the pen while Mr. Prosper figured out a starting bid for each of them. She wouldn't be great when he wanted to see how they ran, but Ryan told her not to worry about that. One of them could switch over to riding if they wanted to check that out.

It occurred to Brynn that she might be a completely unnecessary part of this process, but it was sweet of Ryan to pretend she was doing something to help.

"Okay, great!" Ryan called out to her. "Holt is just pulling up, so I'm gonna go meet him. You okay with hanging out in there until we get back?"

"Sure!" She waved him away, patting the nearest horse.

Ryan disappeared and Brynn turned to the horse beside her. "What are we going to do with these guys, huh? Like standing here with you is going to give me a heart attack."

"I might have a heart attack, I don't know."

There was nothing to do but smile as Ford's mellow voice reached her. She turned to see him leaning on the pen's fence, grinning at her in the most disarming way she'd ever seen.

Good grief, the man was gorgeous.

She swallowed with some difficulty, given how dry her mouth went at the thought. "Why's that?"

He shrugged. "Beautiful woman hanging out with a bunch of horses. The way to my heart, right there."

"I thought that was ribs," Brynn replied with a small smile, more to try and settle her heart while they talked about nothing.

"That, too." He winked and straightened at the fence. "What are you doing?"

She stroked the soft, sun-warmed coat of the horse. "Pretty much babysitting the horses until Ryan and his cousin get back. I think I'm parading them around so Mr. Prosper can decide on a price."

Ford nodded his understanding. "Makes sense. Stock auction is tomorrow, and he stands to make a lot of money, if he does it right."

"But these are his horses, right? Wouldn't he already have an idea of a price to ask?"

"Sure, but you can't submit a price that far in advance. So there's a drill of doing a pre-auction evaluation by the seller. Pretty routine, and not everyone does it. Holt's about as honest as they come, though, so he always does one." Ford hopped over the fence and came over to her, almost sauntering. "I thought I'd help with that."

Brynn bit her lip as he came closer. "I thought Ryan was just taking pity on me because I wanted something to do. Helping with this is a real thing?"

Ford laughed softly, reaching out to tuck a lock of her hair behind her ear. "There's lots of ways to help. I'm pretty good with horses and sales, so I thought I'd help him figure out the numbers. You and Ryan can do the details with the horses themselves. Deal?"

"Whatever you say, Boy Scout."

He leaned in and kissed her. It was quick, but he somehow managed to make her tingle everywhere when he did so. "I say you're the most beautiful woman on this ranch," he murmured.

Her face flamed and she ducked her chin in embarrassment. "Knock it off. Ryan will be back any minute."

"Just thought you should know," Ford told her simply. "It's a fact." He started backing away, giving her a thorough look.

"That's called an opinion," she insisted, propping a hand on her hip.

His crooked grin returned. "It's a fact that it's my opinion. Which is what counts here anyway."

She wouldn't refute that, but why did he have to say it at all? It was making her all buzzing and electrified, and she just wanted to take one of the ATVs with him and ride out into parts of the ranch where no one else was. They could just sit there and watch the sunset or something, and it would be the most perfect day of her life.

Just being with him was enough to make her happy.

Was that enough to mean something?

Ryan appeared then, with a guy who looked enough like him to be related, and he greeted Brynn with a tip of the front of his well-worn hat. Ryan moved into the pen to join her while he and Ford shook hands and chatted for a minute.

She watched as Ford's expression turned to one of surprise, curiosity curling at her insides when Ford nodded and shook the man's hand again.

"What's that about?" she asked when Ryan was close enough.

"Hmm?" He looked where she indicated. "Oh. I was telling Holt the other day how Ford is keeping his eye out for a farm or ranch of his own. Turns out one of his neighbors is getting ready to sell, but doesn't want to deal with the hassle of the whole market if he can find a good man or woman to sell to directly. I'm willing to bet Holt just pitched it to Ford and offered to take him out to look at it one of these days. And it looks like Ford's interested."

After their conversation the other night, Brynn would have to agree with that. Ford wanted to make plans, and he was looking for a place to start. If this place Holt knew about could work for him, it could ground Ford and be what he needed to think about the rest of his life once the rodeo stuff was done.

That tore at Brynn a little. It was purely selfish, she knew, but if he was ready to make plans, then they weren't in the same place in life. And the truth of it was that she might never be ready to make plans again. That might not matter to him now while he was going from place to place during the rodeo season, but when that was over? It would matter a lot.

What was she going to do about that?

CHAPTER 17

"That's it! That's it!"

"Eight!"

Ford, Eric, and Reid looked at Holt in expectation, holding their breath while Lars and Ryan took care of the bull and Westin picked himself up after his creative dismount.

Holt refused to look up at them for a moment, then gradually did so. "If that's not a perfect score, then I've never seen one." He grinned at them, which was rare enough for Holt Prosper, and it only added to the moment.

They erupted in cheers, and Westin pumped a fist in victory. He'd scored a perfect hundred, which was a rarity for bull riders, for the first time not that long ago, and he'd gotten a decent injury in the process. So now he was hungry to get a perfect score without getting hurt, and he was definitely on track to do that.

It was strange how such a victory for one of them seemed like a victory for each of them. They hadn't technically been teammates for years, but that feeling of union between them hadn't left even after all this time.

"I'm gonna end my day on top," Westin told them all, raising a hand and grinning. "That's it for me. Who's up next?"

"Ford wants to go," Reid said at once.

That earned him a look from Ford. "Do I?"

Reid nodded fervently and gestured toward the makeshift arena on Ryan's property. "Yes, you do. Come on, let's see if you can get to three-five."

Ford whistled low, shaking his head. "No pressure or anything." He slapped the rail of the pen and turned to saddle up his horse. The others got a steer ready for him, and Ryan got himself into position to be his hazer.

Trotting over to his chute, Ford caught sight of Shay heading in to join them. "Oh, great," he muttered, shaking his head.

"I heard that!" his sister called out. She took up position next to Reid, who dropped a friendly arm around her shoulder. "Let's go, Motor."

There were snickers from the guys as Ford rode into position, and he tried to tune them all out as he prepped for his run. There was nothing worse than being distracted when he had a chance at a good run. It was bad enough to have a woman stuck in his head, but when he had stupid things like the laughter of idiots and his sister in his head, everything was just compounded into something much, much worse.

This was only a practice run, thank goodness, but the rodeo events started tomorrow night, and he needed to be ready for them.

After this, he'd be back on the road for a few weeks, hitting up a few other rodeos, and while the vacation time, so to speak, had been welcome, he wasn't used to having it. He had been spending the rodeo months driving from place to place every week or so, sometimes every other, and being in one place for so long was starting to make him antsy.

Full Rigged

Kind of like being at home.

It was a strange thing, never being comfortable in one place for long. It made him question his long-term prospects in any place or with anyone. He had no doubt that when the time came, he'd be ready to stop, but all of that would hinge on having somewhere to go.

Or someone to go with.

The image of Brynn popped into his head, just as she had looked earlier in the day. Hair loosely braided and hanging over her shoulder, standing in her jeans and a T-shirt in a pen with horses, looking as content as anyone he'd ever seen. He'd teased her a little about it, but until that moment, he hadn't been entirely sure how Brynn would have done on a ranch or a farm long-term instead of just for a few weeks.

Now he felt certain that she would be just fine.

Which made him want to find that place he could call home even more.

Not that he needed to do so now, or even in the next few days, but he might as well put out feelers. Holt's offer to take him out to Prosper to look at the property he mentioned was pretty near perfect in its timing, and they were already discussing the pair of them heading out after Lost Creek Days ended to see if it was something he'd be interested in.

The idea of staying in Texas one day was an appealing one. He loved this state, and it would be a great place to raise a family someday. If he ever got around to it. And having a farm of his own, a place where he could make the decisions and take the blame, where he could work himself to the bone and see the rewards of it . . .

That would be heaven on earth.

"Set?" Holt called from his position, breaking Ford out of his not-so-focused mind.

Still, Ford nodded, trying to zone in quickly.

Neat lines, fast pace, quick takedown.

Simple enough.

He tightened his hold on the reins, his heels set against his horse, who stirred restlessly with the pressure.

The chute beside him opened, and Ryan and the steer took off. A moment later, Ford was free as well, and he shot off after them, the horse thundering like a storm cloud as they gained on the steer.

He barely registered the cheers and whistles of the others, his eyes set on the steer. He turned in his saddle as they approached the horns, and he threw himself from the horse as his hands gripped the horns tightly. The force of his motion rocked the steer in Ford's direction, its feet flying out from beneath him.

It was a smooth, fluid motion, something perfect in its pattern, and Ford's heart lit up with the elation of such a feeling.

That was cut short as something sharp lanced across his brow, searing pain across his face.

There was one heartbeat, then two, and then the rush of sound from the others hit him in a wave, whistling in celebration.

"Three-six!" Lars cried out, his voice hoarse in his excitement. "Three-six, man! That was poetry!"

Ford released the steer, realizing belatedly that his left hand had slipped from its hold at some point, which allowed the steer to rear back just enough to catch him with that horn. He rolled to his side, hissing as he reached up to touch the pulsing spot on his brow.

"Oh, shoot," he heard Shay exclaim. A subsequent shuffling and thudding told him she'd vaulted the fence and was heading for him.

One or two of the guys cursed, but Ford kept all of his cursing in his head, as usual.

"Stay still, stay still," Shay urged as she got to him.

"It's just a cut," he assured her, scowling in frustration. "Lost my hold on the left horn."

"Rookie mistake," they said together out of sheer habit.

They shared a quick smile before Shay gave him a worried look. "That looks awful. You'll need a doctor." She pulled her bandana from around her neck and folded it, pressing it against his brow, which sent a burning fury into his head.

"I'll call Doc Mills," Ryan told him, jumping down from his horse.

Ford waved him off. "Don't bother him. Just get Brynn, she can take care of this."

"Perfect," Lars said with a nod. "Does she do stitches?"

"I have no idea," Ford retorted. "But she'll tell me if I need them."

"You'll need them," at least three people said at once.

Ford growled under his breath. "Great." He reached up to press his hand against the bandana in place of Shay. "Come on, help me up. I'm not sitting here in the dirt while we wait for her."

Shay tugged him upright with his free hand and walked with him out of the pen. "Maybe we ought to take you up to the house," she suggested. "Cleaner there, and she'll probably want to get you cleaned up before she really gets into stitching."

He gave his sister a dark look. "Can we try to clean me up a little bit here first? I'd love to not look like a bear attacked my face when I see her."

There was zero sympathy in Shay's face. "No, just like a steer's horn got you because you didn't have your head in the game before you ran it. Brynn's not just an impartial doctor looking at your cut—she's also special to you, and she has never seen you ride in an actual rodeo. This is a helluva way to introduce her to this sport you love."

"Injuries are rare in my event," Ford protested, despite his chest clenching. "You know that."

"Sure, and nobody can stop you officially from going back in after one," Shay retorted as they moved to the side of the barn, leaning against it. "But I'm not the one you've got to explain that to. So maybe having your girlfriend stitch you up isn't the brightest idea you've ever had. Now shut up before I stop caring." She folded her arms, looking away.

Ford pressed his tongue to the front of his teeth, thinking that over. Shay was right, as usual, and what he could brush off fairly easily might be a big deal to this woman who was technically not his girlfriend, but very well could be if he played his cards right. But she was a doctor. Surely, she'd seen injuries and the like in her training, if not in her practice.

Did he want her to be the one to stitch him up? Or did he want her to recommend he go to the clinic in Lost Creek for this injury?

Ultimately, he wanted to see her first, whether she treated him medically or not.

So the process was probably still the same.

Ryan came around the corner of the barn, smiling at the siblings. "Brynn's good to go, says she can take care of stitches easily enough. Shay, can you drive him over to the house? ATV or truck, doesn't matter."

Shay grunted once. "ATV. Let this idiot feel the bumps on the drive." She looked at him quickly. "You don't have a headache, do you?"

"No . . ." he said slowly, wondering why she would ask.

"Seeing double? Feeling dizzy?"

He gave her a look. "No, I'm just bleeding."

"Good. No concussion, then. ATV." She waved him to follow her as she strode off toward the line of them.

Full Rigged

Ford followed, rolling his eyes for Ryan's benefit, making his friend laugh as he did so. He got on the ATV behind Shay, holding onto her with one arm while he kept pressure on his cut with the other hand.

She didn't say much as she drove, but she was pretty stiff to the touch. Had she been concerned about the injury and just lashed out at him instead? She had vaulted the fence to get to him, after all.

Maybe he had been too stubborn, too quick to brush off his injury, even though the odds were that it was nothing.

He wasn't really used to people caring that much. Not that people didn't care, but he'd just always kept going and not let anything like this become a big deal.

He'd never thought it might be something significant to somebody else.

They arrived at the house just a minute or two later, and Shay pulled up alongside the porch, staying where she was. "Alrighty, off you go. Be nice, okay?"

Ford climbed off and gave her a smile. "I'm always nice."

Shay snorted softly. "Uh-huh."

He leaned in and kissed her brow quickly. "Sorry if I scared you, kid. I really am fine."

She smiled back at him finally. "I know. Doesn't mean it's not scary. Just remember that, okay?"

He nodded obediently, giving her a jaunty salute.

She revved the ATV before taking off on it again, and it faintly occurred to him that she could be going off to ride hellbent all over the ranch just because she had an ATV to play with.

That was a little terrifying, and he might have to warn Kellie and Ryan.

"Come on up, Ford," Brynn said in a slightly strained, very professional voice as she came out of the house with a small bin of supplies. "I've got a first aid station all set up."

He silently went up onto the porch and sat in the chair she indicated, tipping his head back.

Brynn had a smile on her face, but it wasn't the smile he knew and loved. It was fine, and it still showed how beautiful she was, but this was like the smile she'd given him on the first day.

Polite and distant.

He could respect that. For now.

"Okay, I'll have you take that bandana off now," she said in even tones as she put her medical gloves on. "And why don't you tell me what happened?"

He removed the bandana and started telling her the story, pausing for a pained hiss when she began to clean the area.

"Sorry, it is going to sting a bit, but it won't last long." Her smile spread for a moment, still that polite version she probably wore for any average patient. "I'm just using water. It's decently deep, so there will be a few stitches, but it's really clean, all told."

"Okay," he said simply, smiling back at her.

Her smile didn't change. "Do you want anesthetic for the stitching?"

He shook his head. "Nah, I can't feel much up there right now anyway."

She nodded and turned to her kit, pulling out a strange pair of tweezers crossed with scissors and a needle with a long, tough thread attached to it. "Fair enough. Don't move much on me, okay? Otherwise it won't be a pretty scar."

"Well, all I've got is my face, so please make it pretty." He smiled, closing his eyes and trying to relax in the awkward position he sat in.

"You feel like finishing the story?" Brynn asked as her hands rested against his face, a sharp stinging registering in the vicinity of his cut.

"Can I?" he asked, trying not to move his face. "It won't mess you up?"

"Nope. Just don't frown much."

He grinned, though he wouldn't see her reaction to it. "Can do." He went on with his stupid injury story, trying to remember that she didn't understand his sport and that he'd need to explain even the minor details of it.

Since he couldn't see her face, there was no telling if she was in any way interested in what he was saying, but she wasn't shutting him up, so he'd take that as a good sign. She was the sort of person to do so, and was direct enough to admit if she was bored, and unless he was otherwise directed, he'd keep doing whatever she asked him to. If she wanted to hear his story, he'd tell it a dozen times.

"And that's done," she broke in. "I'll just put some topical antibiotic on there, and cover it with some sterile strips and a little patch of gauze I'll tape on. Keep this on tonight, and tomorrow, before you head into Lost Creek, I'll check it and see if we can take the dressings down completely. Don't get it wet."

"Yes, ma'am." He waited for her to finish those last few steps, and when she fully stepped away, he opened his eyes and lifted his head, shifting in his chair to be more comfortable. "That wasn't as bad as I thought. Guess I had a darn good doctor."

"Could be," she said, her voice less careful now than it had been moments ago. "But what were you thinking, honestly? I don't know anything about steer wrestling, but you just told me you had a lot on your mind, so you weren't as ready as you normally are. Why wouldn't you wait until you were ready? This was a practice run with your friends. You could have said you needed a minute. Don't you know how dangerous it is? Even if you aren't always at risk of getting gouged in the face with a horn, you could get crushed underneath the steer, you could lose your footing when you come off the horse, you could..."

"Have you been watching videos of rodeo injuries?" he interrupted with a smile. "That's not a good idea, sweetheart."

She didn't seem to hear him, or if she did, it made no difference. "It's bad enough that you're even doing this crazy stuff, but now you're telling me that you aren't always mentally ready for it. And if you're not mentally ready, how can you be sure you're physically ready? What are the medical services like at the rodeo anyway? Does anybody care if you aren't in any condition to ride? What if I decide tomorrow that your cut isn't okay? Is anyone going to back up my professional opinion and keep you off of a horse?"

Ford watched her spiraling with a little amusement, which was probably terrible of him. "You keep talkin' like that, darlin', and I'm gonna start thinking you like me a little."

Brynn froze, her eyes flicking in his direction, but not quite making it. "And if I do like you?"

His eyes widened, and so did his smile. "That'd be the best thing I've heard in a long time."

She set her tools in the basket and tossed the gauze and tape in after, then stripped off her gloves and tossed those into a waste basket sitting on the porch. Then she pressed her hands onto the surface of the table, her fingers shaking.

Ford watched them for a moment. "You weren't shaking like that when you stitched me, right?"

Brynn shook her head, which only seemed to make her shaking worse. "No. That was Dr. Kershaw, and she was fine, very professional. This is Brynn now, and she was so scared..."

Any amusement he felt vanished completely. "Oh, darlin', come here." He opened his arms, gesturing for her.

She turned to him immediately and crawled onto his lap, nuzzling against him as his arms wrapped around her. One of her hands gripped at his shirt just below his throat, and the other pressed against his heart as though she needed to be sure it was still beating.

"Ryan said you needed a doctor, and I thought I was going to be sick," Brynn whispered, trembling where she sat. "I didn't even see what had happened, and I was seeing all of the injury videos I watched, only your face was on every cowboy I saw. I don't know if I can take this, Ford."

"Take what, sweetheart?" he murmured, kissing her hair and her brow, cradling her head against him. "What can't you take?"

"This," she insisted. "You. Caring about you this much and being terrified of everything you do."

He tucked her head beneath his chin, one hand weaving in and out of her hair soothingly. "Would it help if I tell you that injuries in steer wrestling are rare? Would talking to Shay about it help?"

Brynn shrugged in his hold. "Would it? Does it bother her at all?"

"Sure," he replied at once. "She was royally ticked at me when I tried to brush this off. She's seen me ride hundreds of times, even when I was doing different events with more risk to them. And she's sat by my mom when I've done those. But if that's not going to help you, I won't suggest it."

She was silent for a long moment. "It might help," she admitted softly. "And I'll want to sit by her at the rodeo, too."

He smiled at the image that idea put in his mind. "I think she'd like that. She likes you a lot."

"I like her, too." Brynn fell silent again, and her shaking stopped. She softened against him, curling up almost like a cat by a fire. "Ford . . . I'm scared."

Ford looked down at her, though he couldn't see her eyes. "We just talked about that. You don't have to be, sweetheart. I'm always careful, and there's plenty of help . . ."

"I'm not talking about rodeo."

He pressed his lips together, his mind spinning on that. Fearing the possibilities, he set his lips at her hair, needing as much connection with her as possible. "Then what?"

"This," she murmured, rubbing her hand over his heart. "Us. Feeling so much so fast. I don't know what's happening here, and part of me wants to backpedal until this is somewhere on the map, not on the horizon. Horizons scare me. I can't . . ." She shook her head against him. "You're an all-in guy. That scares me."

If a heart could groan, his did then. "Listen to me, Brynn," he said in a low voice, shifting his hold on her so he could look into her eyes. "Listen, please."

She nodded, an almost desperate light coming into her eyes.

He sighed, cupping her cheek in one hand. "I am an all-in guy. I know that. That doesn't mean I'm an 'all in right now or nothing ever' guy. I respect boundaries and the time it takes for trust and feelings to grow. I know where I'm headed with you, but that doesn't mean you have to know the same thing right this minute. I'm not going anywhere, okay? That's what this means. You take the time you need, and just understand that I'll still be here. And I'm not going to make big statements or ask any scary questions until I'm pretty positive I'm gonna get the answer I want when I do. I'm not going to ask you for forever. I just want tomorrow. Can you give me tomorrow?"

She searched his eyes, the panicked look beginning to fade. He watched her swallow, and his thumb reached over to touch her bottom lip gently. She leaned into his touch and kissed his thumb. "Yeah," she whispered, nodding. "Yeah, I can give you tomorrow."

"Okay," he replied softly. "And can I kiss you now?"

Her sigh echoed his own. "Please do."

He closed the distance between them, his lips taking hers, and she clung to him with an intensity that humbled him to his core. He cradled her as much as she would let him, gave as much as she would take, and received everything she wanted to give him. There was no denying her interest, or her passion, and he knew full well that it was incredible she could even give this much. He was touched by her bravery, and her trust in him already. He'd treasure every moment with her, every kiss and every touch, every embrace and every hurt she confided.

He'd meant every word he'd said.

He wasn't going anywhere.

Chapter 18

Rodeo was insanity. That's what Brynn had decided after the first two nights of it. She'd seen all the guys compete, including Ford, and she'd found herself getting caught up in the energy and excitement of it. Didn't mean she thought any of them were particularly sane for doing so, but she could cheer hard and was learning how to tell a good ride from a great one.

Shay was a fantastic tutor in all of the events, and her calm about everything related to the competition helped to settle every fear Brynn harbored about it.

Shay also knew a ton of great stories about Ford.

Which helped in other ways.

There were no words for how wonderful Ford had been in the last few days, especially where Brynn's uncertainty was concerned. He never pushed, never made her feel as though he was waiting for something, never once showed any kind of impatience or irritation. It was like he was a saint dropped into a cowboy's body and situation, and, apart from how crazy he could make her, and how snarky he and his sister could be together, she wouldn't think he had any flaws at all.

Shay had seemed to decide it was her mission to make sure all of Ford's flaws were known to Brynn, and it made for entertaining conversations. Brynn had only told Ford about half of those conversations, and he'd only laughed and continued to hold her.

He loved to hold her. She wasn't making an assumption there—he'd flat out admitted that from the first day he'd held her, he'd just wanted to do it again.

Since Brynn loved being held by him, it was a pretty convenient detail to discover.

Late night porch-sitting at the homestead house had become their thing the last few nights. Arms around each other while they talked, or just sat and looked at the stars . . . It was the most perfect series of moments she'd ever known in her entire life, and considering she had been through an entire marriage that she'd once adored, that was saying a lot.

And yet . . .

She hadn't been able to stop herself from being afraid. Afraid that she was falling too far, afraid that she was going to disappoint Ford, afraid that she was going to want too much again. Afraid that, despite what he said, he would become tired of waiting for her to be ready.

She might never be ready.

Eventually, she'd have to tell him that.

But not now.

Now, she was getting ready for the final night of rodeo watching, making her way through the crowd at the Lost Creek arena with everyone else who had come out for the last night. Riders had come from all over the place for this, which surprised her, as Lost Creek was not a big town or in any way a major point of interest in the state of Texas, and yet this seemed to be a favorite tradition for a lot of the competitors. All of Lost Creek had to be in the stands, and then some.

Brynn had never felt more like she had been missing out on something in her entire life than she had in the last few days, watching all of this unfold.

And it was contagious.

Even Josie had come out to the rodeo last night, and she was here with them tonight as well. More than that, she was dressed to the cowgirl nines and could not have been more adorable as she cheered for all of her new friends.

Brynn looked behind her now to check on the cute girl, and her amusement faded at once.

Josie had been trapped by a man in denim who towered over her, and one look at her face told Brynn everything she needed to know.

"Paige," she called. "Shay! Trish!" The others were meeting them here, and there was no time for a conference. Brynn marched in Josie's direction, and the girl's wide eyes met hers when she saw her.

"Come on, sweet pea," the guy crooned, reaching for a hand that Josie jerked away from him. "Stop playing hard to get. You're my type, and I always get my type."

"Step away from her, buck," Brynn spat. "Now."

The guy turned, wearing a drunken, cocky smirk. "Hey, spitfire. I'll take a taste of you when I'm done with her."

"You're done now," Brynn barked. "Josie, go."

Josie scurried away, and the guy started after her, but Brynn blocked him.

He looked down at her with a snarl that soon curled into a sneer. "Fine. I'll just have you."

"Don't touch me," Brynn ordered, fury roaring within her almost on command. "Where do you get off, you disgusting, perverted, arrogant pig of a man? How dare you antagonize a woman like you just did to my friend just because you can't decide which part of you actually houses your brain?! Did you ever have manners, or were they slapped out of you by every woman in your life? You lack every single moral and respectable quality that I have discovered to be in the men of this town, and the guys riding in the rodeo. You are nothing but a bug, and I will crush you beneath my boot if you so much as look at my friend again. I'm gonna give you three seconds to tuck in that pitiful tail and turn around and walk away. Walk far away. Walk out of this arena, and away from this place."

He took a step toward her, expression murderous, but Brynn was headed into full surge now, and he had nothing on that.

"Get out," she said slowly, glowering at him. "Do not test me, or so help me, I will end you in ways you cannot even begin to imagine. And I know way too many people who hold a lot of sway here to give you a whiff of hope if you don't do what I say right now."

His hands clenched and unclenched at his sides, then he spat on the ground and turned on his heel, storming out.

Brynn exhaled shortly and pulled out her phone, hitting two buttons to place a call. "Ryan? I don't know who's in charge, but there's a denim-clad ogre in a dirty, white cowboy hat headed for the east gate. Six-three, two-seventy, unshaven, clearly drunk. He tried something with Josie and with me, and I just ticked him off. Okay, thanks."

Hanging up, she dropped her phone in her back pocket and turned back to her friends, all of whom stared at her with wide eyes.

Shay cleared her throat. "Remind me, Doc, what it is you're at the ranch for."

"Anger management issues," Brynn told her, still fuming. She looked around at them, and her anger slowly ebbed away. She cracked a smile, then burst out laughing at what had just happened, and what she'd just done.

"That was amazing." Josie gushed, rushing to give her a hug. "He was so much taller than you, and you just let him have it! Oh my gosh, you're my hero."

"Mine, too." Trish praised with a high five. "I think my hero here deserves a drink."

They made their way to the concession stand, got some drinks and food, and moved to their seats in the stands.

The more Brynn thought about her outburst with Big Ugly Creep, the more troubled she got. Yes, she'd done the right thing by intervening, and yes, he deserved to be told off, but she'd acted completely out of anger, and let that anger ride within her just when she'd been trying to figure out how to be angry without getting a surge-level dose of it. And here she'd just ripped it open like a bad wound, practically embracing the experience because she could actually use it this time. Couldn't control it, really, but she could use it.

Did that make things any better?

She sat in the stands while they waited for the events to start, and soon Kellie, Meredith, and Julia joined them. She had no doubt they'd be told the story, probably incorrectly, and it was entirely possible Kellie would want to talk to her about that, considering she would know the signs of how Brynn surged.

They'd talked about it enough, and even named the stages.

Now she was in the final stage. Letdown. And with that stage came the regret, the guilt, the insecurity, and the exhaustion.

Had she not been looking forward to watching Ford again and seeing if he could meet his goals, she would have gone home and gone right to bed.

There was nothing else to do except that.

The first events passed like a blur to her, sitting and stewing as she was in letdown. She needed to put it aside, needed to focus on having fun tonight, as all of the others were doing. They had planned tonight to be a celebration of Lost Creek and their time in it, and she would be in no state to do so if she kept sitting in this moping reflection.

"Need to talk?" Kellie asked as she sat beside her.

Brynn gave her a look. "How'd you know?"

"I've been at this a while," her friend replied with a fond smile. "And we've been talking long enough that I figured. What's got you stuck?"

"I surged," Brynn whispered, afraid to admit it too loudly. "I don't want to surge, and I've been so good."

Kellie wet her lips and took Brynn's hand in her own. "I heard the story, Brynn. I don't think you surged at all. I think you got mad. Which seems right, under the circumstances. You didn't have a crazy build-up that made no sense. You didn't lose control. You didn't feel like tearing the arena down. You got mad because your friend was in a bad situation. And you acted. You know what that makes you?"

"An angry mess?" Brynn suggested dryly.

"Human."

That was a surprising answer, and Brynn stared at Kellie in shock.

Kellie nodded at her disbelief. "Human, Brynn. You can be angry—that isn't a problem. You were able to come down out of your anger when you were back with your friends, and when you knew everyone was safe. This wasn't irrational, this wasn't a volcano that needed to erupt before you hurt someone. This was just you, and you can be angry. Humans get angry."

"They do, don't they?" Brynn shook her head, feeling oddly warm at the realization.

"And you know what else?"

"What?"

Kellie squeezed her hand. "Even if you had surged, that would have been okay. It's not falling off the wagon. It's a process, and processes have bumps. Don't beat yourself up, okay?"

"Are you sure I'm not in letdown from a surge?" Brynn asked, afraid to completely give in to the hope that was pressing against her chest.

"Pretty sure," Kellie returned with a wink. "I'm not in your head, but I think you're just feeling guilty for getting mad, and guilt can spiral a lot like letdown. You're okay, Brynn. I promise."

Brynn managed a smile at that, and hugged her friend and therapist tightly. "Thank you."

"You're welcome." Kellie rubbed her back, then pulled away with a smile. "Be kind to yourself. Rule number four."

"Is that written somewhere?" Brynn asked her with a furrowed brow.

She nodded, rising to climb back up to her seat behind her. "Yep. Kellie's Ranch Rules. It's on the back of my door."

Brynn reared back at that. "Who's going to see it back there?"

Kellie raised a brow. "I am, of course." She grinned and turned her attention to the first event of the evening.

It took Brynn a bit longer to focus, but eventually, she was able to tune back in and cheer for Reid as he competed in the insanity that was bareback bronc riding.

After he escaped without injury, and with a score that was good, though she didn't understand how, it was time for the steer wrestling.

Her heart jumped into her throat and would not budge, no matter how she swallowed or cleared her throat.

She watched every competitor before Ford, her fingernails digging into her palms as she curled her hands into hard fists of nerves.

Please let him be safe. Please let him be safe.

"What's he doing right now?" Brynn whispered to Shay. "What's his pre-ride process?"

Shay's left leg was bouncing anxiously in her seat. "He's been watching every rider go, standing with his arms folded and taking mental notes. He'll remember the time of every guy before him, but it doesn't affect his psyche. He's not competing with them, he's competing with the clock. He doesn't care. He likes to see how they ride and what their technique is. It won't change how he rides tonight, but he might practice new tricks tomorrow. Since it's almost his turn, he'll be standing over by the chute, away from everyone else, and doing a run in his head."

Brynn tried to picture it, could almost see Ford staring off at nothing, visualizing his run, stoic and ready to go.

He could do this. He could absolutely do this.

Of course, he could do this. The man had been doing this, and she'd watched him do it two nights in a row. Why in the world would tonight be any different?

Shay exhaled slowly, bringing Brynn's attention up. Ford's name was on the board now, and she looked down at the arena quickly.

Time seemed to slow as she watched. Ryan and the steer were suddenly loose, Ryan riding by its side, just like he was supposed to do. Then Ford came bolting out of the chute, looking powerful and intense, completely attuned to the steer and its progress. It was amazing to watch how he could keep riding when his hands were free, then suddenly lurch off and grab the steer by the horns.

The steer flipped almost at once, its feet flopping in the same direction.

Ford jumped up, completely unharmed, which made Brynn's heart settle enough to look over at the clock.

Shay started screaming beside her, and the crowd around her erupted, but Brynn could only blink at the time.

Three-point-four-two.

Three-point-four seconds. Everybody who had gone so far had been a low four or a high three. Ford had told her he wanted to get a three-point-five-second time this season, but he wasn't sure he'd get there.

He'd just gone beyond that.

Stunned, Brynn looked down at him, slowly rising to her feet.

Ford had already headed out, but when the announcer reiterated that Ford had just broken the arena record, the officials had him go back into the ring and take a wave for the crowd.

He raised a hand in greeting, acknowledging the cheers, his face fairly impassive, though he did wear a tightlipped smile. When the crowd only cheered louder, he took his hat off and gestured a bow with it before putting it back on his head and patting his heart in thanks. Then he turned in their direction, and his eyes found her and Shay.

He broke out into a broad grin, kissed two fingers, and pointed them up at them.

There was nothing like that to make Brynn want to rush down there and kiss him in front of everybody here.

And that was terrifying.

She wanted that? She wanted to stake her claim on him?

What did that mean? How far beyond tomorrow was she willing to go? All Ford ever asked her was to give him tomorrow, and she always agreed. Tomorrow was easy enough.

Did she want more than tomorrow? She knew that he did, but did she?

That was almost impossible to say at this point.

"Come on," Shay hissed, tugging at her hand.

Full Rigged

"What?" Brynn resisted a little. "Where are we going?"

Shay gave her a bewildered look. "Where do you think? We're going down there to congratulate him!"

Brynn went slack-jawed and her resistance vanished. "We can do that?" she asked as she followed.

"Heck yeah." Shay grinned over her shoulder as they walked up the stairs to the concourse level. "He just broke a record, and he's gonna want to see you."

"And you," Brynn pointed out.

Shay snorted a laugh. "If you think kissing two fingers means two kisses, one for you and one for me, you need your head checked, Doc. If he did something for me, it would be an air five or something. Promise."

That didn't help Brynn's shaking knees, but she didn't say anything else as they hurried down the concourse and found their way down to the arena floor level. There were cowboys and horses everywhere, and officials and clowns wove through them all with ease. Not one person seemed to care that they were down here.

How were they going to find him?

Shay suddenly let out a whistle in a songbird sort of fashion, making Brynn jump. More startling still was a response that was almost as musical as hers had been.

"What in the world?" Brynn laughed, her hand still tight in Shay's.

"Gotta be able to find each other in crowds," Shay explained. "We all do it." She suddenly released Brynn's hand and took off at a run. "Hey!"

Brynn watched as Shay was swept up in Ford's arms in a bear hug that made her smile. They were laughing and ruffling each other's hair, and it seemed a shame to interrupt that for something else.

But Ford looked her direction, his face still wreathed in

elation that he hadn't shown as much for the public. That he showed it to her was overwhelming.

He moved in her direction and pulled her into his arms in a less enthusiastic but no less touching manner.

Brynn pulled back and kissed him, gripping his neck tightly before touching her brow to his. "Congrats, Boy Scout."

He grinned and kissed her again, clearly still full of the rush of victory. "Hey, listen," he said, dropping his voice a little lower. "I gotta go watch the rest of the Six knock tonight out. Tomorrow, I'm going out to Prosper to look at that property Holt told me about. I want you to come with me."

A cold wave washed over Brynn as she stared at him, her heartbeat seeming to slow. "Why?"

Ford raised a brow, still smiling. "Why? Because I love you, Brynn Kershaw, and when the day comes that it's safe enough to ask you a question, I want to know that you like the place where I'm going to live."

She gaped at him, blinking in disbelief. "I can't."

His smile faded, and he took her hand. "Can't what? Can't come with me? Can't answer a question I didn't ask? Can't reply with something I haven't expected?" He paused, giving her a long look. "Can't be with me at all?"

Brynn swallowed hard. "I can't promise more than tomorrow. And I can't come with you to Prosper because I can't promise more than tomorrow. I can't say anything more, whether you ask or expect or not. And I need to know if that's good enough."

Ford stared at her, saying nothing for a minute, and she could see the disappointment in his eyes. But she also saw something else.

Love.

"I'm not going anywhere, Brynn," he said firmly, moving

his hand to her upper arm. "And if I've rushed things, I'm sorry. I'm going to Prosper tomorrow. If I don't hear from you, I'll keep going to my next rodeo destination. Not to leave you, but to keep moving like my career demands. I'll be whatever you want me to be, Brynn. You just let me know." He leaned in to kiss her brow, then turned and headed back through the crowd, giving his sister a high five as he passed her, his head down.

She couldn't say anything, and he was okay with that?

Why wasn't she okay with that?

CHAPTER 19

PROSPER, TEXAS, WAS AS gorgeous as Lost Creek, Texas, and he'd tell anybody who cared to listen.

Ford could easily see himself living in this town and taking an active part in it.

The question was whether or not the land he was going to see would be something he wanted to work, and if he could see the potential in it. If he could see himself there.

If he could see Brynn there.

He shook his head to himself as he drove, Sherlock panting heavily beside him, sticking his head between the seats just as he always did.

There was no point in asking himself if he could see Brynn on the land with him. She had given him no promises that she was in any way interested in what he had to offer in the future. He could respect that, given what she had been through. Should have expected that.

But heaven help him, he wanted a future with her.

He wanted her to want a future with him.

Maybe he didn't mean it when he said he would wait as

long as it took. Maybe he only meant for as long as he could hold out hope.

Even as he said that, he knew it wasn't right.

He wanted Brynn Kershaw. And if Brynn Kershaw needed five years, he'd give her five years. If she needed ten years, he'd give her ten years. If she needed longer . . .

Then he needed longer, too.

His mother would never understand that. She wanted Ford to bring home a girl with a ring on her finger tomorrow, if possible, but he knew that she was only worried about his happiness and his future prospects. He wanted to settle down one day, too.

Maybe it mattered less where he hung his hat at the end of the day, and it mattered more who was with him when he did.

Home could be anywhere if Brynn was there.

Maybe he needed to tell her that.

Or maybe he needed to say less. In the exhilaration of his record-setting night, he'd told her that he loved her. That was true, but it was also something he hadn't exactly planned on revealing so soon. He chalked it up to some insane confidence after his win, or a stupid side effect of adrenaline, but it was bad timing on his part, there was no question.

Honestly, he was lucky Brynn hadn't run from him when he'd said it.

She was a classic example of commitment issues, and those weren't her fault. Pushing too hard, wanting too much, was the surest way to run her out of town, and with everything she had told him, he ought to have remembered that.

They hadn't sat together on the porch last night, and he hadn't seen her this morning before he left. Hadn't heard from her.

He'd packed up with the expectation that he would be

heading down to San Antonio after this to get ready for the next rodeo on the circuit. He couldn't operate under any other understanding after the conversation he'd had with Brynn last night.

And if he had to do that, so be it. He'd just call Brynn tonight from San Antonio, or maybe tomorrow, and make sure she was okay. Validate her feelings. Accept her concerns.

The only way she could believe that he meant what he said would be for him to do exactly what he said. If he were always there for her, she would see that he could be believed and trusted in the way she was most afraid to believe and trust.

He had all the time in the world to prove to her that he did love her, and that because he loved her, he would stay by her.

But those words might not mean the same to her as they did to him.

Her ex might have taken the power out of them.

He could add that to the list of things to want to kill the guy for.

He pulled into the drive labeled with the name and numbers Holt had given him, heading down the gravel road until he saw Holt standing by his truck waiting for him.

Ford parked beside him and got out, opening the door for Sherlock, who immediately started bounding off to enjoy his freedom from the truck.

"Morning," Holt greeted, pushing off of his truck. "Ready?"

"Yep." Ford shook his hand, nodding firmly. "I'll make this quick. Don't want to keep you from your Sunday."

"Macie's not expecting me until supper," Holt assured him with a quick smile. "We've got lots of time to see whatever you want about the place. This isn't the kind of decision you make on limited information, you know that. I chatted with

Bob already this morning, and he'd like you to take a good look at everything before coming inside to talk with him. Since you're a ranch man yourself, he figures it'll give you better questions to ask him."

Ford frowned a little. "Why do I feel like I'm about to get tested on something?"

Holt gave him zero comfort in his expression. "You probably are, to be honest. Bob's pretty serious about only selling to someone who will love and work the place as much as he does. Doesn't have to be the same work, just the same effort."

"I can respect that. My father would be the same way." Ford snorted once, shaking his head. "He is the same way. My brother feels like he's having to prove himself over and over, even though it's already been decided that he's taking over."

"Funny how that works, huh?" Holt said with a rueful smile. "So just you? Ryan told me you might bring your lady friend, too."

Ford kept his expression impassive. "Just me. She wanted to stay back in Lost Creek. Can't say I blame her; it was a late night."

Holt chuckled and clapped him on the back. "Sure was, record holder." He jerked his head toward the ranch. "Let's check it out."

They had started to walk in that direction when the gravel behind them crunched with the telltale sound of tires. "You expecting someone else?" Ford asked Holt in surprise. "Another prospect?"

Holt frowned, shaking his head. "Bob hasn't even made it public that he's eventually selling." He turned to look behind them, then his expression cleared. "You sure she wanted to stay in Lost Creek, Ford?"

"What?" Ford turned, looking at Kellie Prosper's truck as it pulled in beside him, only it wasn't Kellie behind the wheel.

It was Brynn.

He gaped, actually needing the nudge from Holt to start walking toward her.

"I'll be inside chatting with Bob," Holt told him, laughing. "Come get me when this is all settled and you're ready to take a look."

Ford waved a hand in acknowledgment, not willing to look away from the sight he was seeing to reply.

He couldn't look away.

Brynn hopped down from the truck, pushing her sunglasses on top of her head, looking like the sunrise to him, even if her expression was a little concerned.

She'd always be the most beautiful sight.

She didn't say anything as he approached, and she didn't walk toward him.

Despite the fact that she was here, that scared him.

He swallowed against his parched throat when he got close enough to talk without shouting. "What are you doing here?"

Brynn smiled hesitantly. "I was invited, right?"

"Yeah . . ." He wet his lips carefully. "You weren't interested before."

Her expression tightened, but her smile remained. "Well . . . Dr. Kershaw needed to check her patient's stitches and see how they're doing. She wanted to make sure everything is okay."

His heart skipped at the division of herself again. Would Brynn want more or less than Dr. Kershaw had? Who had done the driving?

Who was he talking to now?

"And Brynn?" he asked, holding his breath. "What does Brynn want?"

"Brynn wants . . ." She paused, fidgeting and looking

down at her fingers before clearing her throat and meeting his eyes. "I want . . ."

Something she saw in him made her soften, and she shook her head. "You."

He exhaled in a rush, unable to move, unable to think.

Brynn smiled a soft, almost watery smile. "I love you. And I want you today, tomorrow, the day after tomorrow, and quite possibly forever. I spent all night thinking it over, and I don't think I'll be happy with only promising tomorrow with you. Maybe I'm not quite ready to commit to forever, but I'm more ready today than I was yesterday. I'm willing to try. I'm headed in that direction, and I'm okay with that. I'm really hoping that's enough."

Ford stared at this woman, this amazing, remarkable, powerful woman who was able to take a chance when she had endured so much hurt. Who could take this step out into the darkness for him when she had spent so long in darkness someone else had thrust upon her.

How could he not love her and want her forever?

His lack of answer clearly unsettled Brynn, and she bit her lip. "Is it enough?"

He swallowed and strode over to her. "It's more than enough. I love you."

She sighed a half-sob and rushed at him, throwing her arms around his neck and kissing him hard. He hauled her against him, kissing her back with just as much energy, craving the touch and taste of her more than anything he'd craved in his life, and never getting enough of her. Every pass of her lips was sweeter, every hint of her scent more divine, every touch of her fingers more electrifying.

He'd never want more than this. More than her.

Brynn sighed as she broke off from one of their thousand kisses. "I was terrified you were going to say you weren't interested."

"I could be dead and still be interested," he assured her, nudging her jaw with his nose and kissing a spot softly. "How'd you get the address?"

"Kellie called Macie," she moaned as he dusted kisses along her neck. "Said if you said no, she'd disown you from the adoptive family."

Ford laughed against her skin. "Well, we couldn't have that. But I don't need her threats or any bribes to say yes. I love you, and that's not going away."

Brynn sighed and gave him a long, slow kiss. "That's good. Because I also brought berry streusel muffins, and I really didn't want to share."

"On second thought . . ."

"What?" she laughed, slapping his shoulder. "I thought I was enough!"

Ford kissed her then, a soft, featherlight kiss. "You are more than enough. I'm just willing to bet you taste even more amazing after or in between one of those muffins, and I think we need to find out."

Brynn's laughter rippled across the sky and wrapped around his heart. And when she let him pick her up and wrapped her legs around him, bringing them on eye level, still kissing each other as though tomorrow would never come, he knew that, whatever he thought of this land or this place, he was home.

With her in his arms, he was home.

Epilogue

"Ford! Shay's on your cell. She wants to argue about your tux."

Ford groaned from his stool, pausing his saddle cleaning process as he looked up at the gorgeous honey-haired woman standing in the door of his barn. "I'm not interested in a tux. I told her I'd get a suit, and that's as far as I'll go."

Brynn folded her arms, the ring on her hand catching the afternoon light in a way that almost lit up the whole barn. "Ford Hopkins, your sister is getting married, and you will wear whatever she wants you to wear."

He made a face, groaning for what had to be the hundredth time since this conversation had started two months ago. "Tuxes are for grooms, darlin'. Not for brothers of the bride. She's probably getting married in that barn she sent us pictures of. Tuxes don't belong in a barn!"

"For someone who hates fashion, you sure seem to know a lot about tuxes." Brynn raised a brow.

He gave her a warning look. "Nope. You didn't make me wear a tux on our wedding day, therefore I don't have to wear one on Shay's."

"Are you telling me I could have asked you to wear a tux and you'd have said yes?" his wife asked, leaning against the barn door in a way that made her adorable baby bump stick out farther than it already did. He thought it was the most beautiful sight he'd ever seen; Brynn thought it was outrageous.

Their discussions on the topic always ended well no matter which side they took.

Ford smiled reluctantly at her. "I'd have worn anything you asked if it meant you'd say 'I do' at the right time."

She smiled back and nodded in approval. "Darn right. I had to keep you guessing."

"But I would have grumbled about a tux later," he added as an afterthought.

"Ford!" Brynn rolled her eyes and came over to him. "I don't care. The point is that you need to talk to her, not me. Come on." She held out a hand, giving him a hard look.

Muttering incoherently, Ford took her hand and pushed up from the stool, pausing a moment to give his beautiful wife a long, thorough kiss that had her shivering in his arms.

"I love it when you do that," she murmured with a sigh.

He chuckled and kissed her brow. "I love doing that." He looked down at her, putting a hand to her cheek. "You sure you want to work tonight? You've been going nonstop lately."

Brynn patted his chest, smiling. "It's my last shift on call before maternity leave. After tonight, there's just a month to go of clinic. I feel great, I really do. Better than I have lately, despite being the size of a heifer."

"No offense, love," Ford told her with a grimace, "but if you were a heifer and you were this size, it would be really, really bad. You're supposed to be a lot bigger than you as a heifer expecting a calf, or else the calf doesn't have a chance."

His wife blinked at his explanation. "That is oddly

comforting. Thanks, babe." She kissed him quickly, tugging on his hand. "Enough procrastinating. Let's go."

He laughed as she pulled him out of the barn, knowing he could easily scoop her up and entertain them both in better ways that would have nothing to do with sisters or tuxes, but finding it cute when she was a little irritated with him.

Just a little.

She'd come so far from the woman he'd fallen for at Broken Hearts Ranch, and he'd loved watching her grow and heal and learn to trust herself again. She still went back every now and then to check in on the new guests, as well as to visit Kellie, and she was still in touch with all of the women who had been with her during her time there.

Only a few months ago, she'd been a bridesmaid for Josie when she'd married the most gentle-hearted policeman Ford had ever met. The guy could also outshoot Ford, which made Ford feel a little better about him.

Every now and then, Brynn still got stressed out enough to surge, but the surges were so small compared to what they had once been, and so long as he was around to hold her tightly, she managed them without much of a blip on the radar.

Now they were expecting a baby in a month, and they could not be more excited about it. Brynn was adamant that they were not finding out the gender, and Ford had gone along with it. He didn't have a preference one way or the other, as each would have benefits in different ways. He just wanted a healthy baby that he could teach how to ride a horse, rope a calf, and wrestle a steer.

When he or she was old enough, of course.

He'd start planning from day one, though.

They entered the house, which they had just finished renovating after purchasing it from Bob. It had taken a lot longer than they'd anticipated, fixing things up and making this place their home, but it had been worth it. Their blood and sweat were in these walls now, and maybe a few of Brynn's tears, but only because Ford had tickled her until she cried.

He refused to make her cry out of sadness or anger or hurt. So far, he'd been successful there.

Once inside, Brynn picked up his cell and handed it to him with a scolding look. "Talk. Don't fight."

He gave her an innocent look. "I never fight."

"Uh-huh." She went up on her tiptoes and kissed him. "Love you."

"Love you, too." He winked and watched her head to the garage, waited for the sound of the engine, and for the garage door to come back down.

Only then did he put the phone to his ear. "Shay?"

"Good gravy, how long does it take you to get to the phone?" his sister barked.

"I had to put up a fight about the tux again," he reminded her. "And then Brynn left to go to work. It's her last shift on call before the baby."

Shay huffed in pretend irritation. "Fine, keeping up the cover story is a good excuse. I've got everything set up with Mom and Carly, and Brynn's mom is coming, too. Kellie's coming with Mariah, and yes, they're bringing your stupid muffins."

"Take that back," Ford insisted half-heartedly. "They'll hear you."

"Whatever. Everyone else on the list is either coming or has sent presents to me already. We are a go. All you've got to do is make sure that Brynn will be home next Saturday. Can you handle that?"

Ford considered the task of keeping his wife at home so she could be surprised with the most epic baby shower his sister could dream up, and showered with all of the love and attention that she would never have thought herself worthy of.

She was going to kill him for this. But then she would cry in his arms about how sweet it was, and how amazing people were, and how she'd love him forever, and he'd be able to hold her for hours.

Maybe the epic baby shower was actually for him.

"Yep," he told his sister as a wide grin crossed his face. "I can handle that."

Roosters Baked Skillet Mac and Cheese

1 lb. dried elbow pasta
1/2 cup unsalted butter
1/2 cup all-purpose flour
1 1/2 cups whole milk
2 1/2 cups half and half
2 cups cheddar cheese
1 cup Colby cheese, shredded
1 cup Muenster cheese, shredded
1 1/2 cups Gruyere cheese, shredded
1/2 cup mozzarella cheese, shredded
1/2 Tbsp. salt
1/2 tsp. black pepper
1/4 tsp. paprika
*Additional mix-in toppings as desired
**You can use any blend of cheeses of your choice.
The total amounts should be the same. ALWAYS shred the cheese yourself!

Bread Crumb Topping

1 cup crushed Ritz crackers
2 tablespoons unsalted butter, melted

Instructions

Preheat oven to 325°F and grease a 3 qt baking dish (9x13"). Set aside.

Bring a large pot of salted water to a boil. When boiling, add dried pasta and cook 1 minute less than the package directs for al dente. Drain and drizzle with a little bit of olive oil to keep from sticking.

While water is coming up to a boil, grate cheeses and toss together to mix, then divide into three piles. Approximately 3 cups for the sauce, 1 1/2 cups for the inner layer, and 1 1/2 cups for the topping.

Melt butter in a large saucepan over MED heat. Sprinkle in flour and whisk to combine. Mixture will look like very wet sand. Cook for approximately 1 minute, whisking often. Slowly pour in about 2 cups or so of the milk/half and half, while whisking constantly, until smooth. Slowly pour in the remaining milk/half and half, while whisking constantly, until combined and smooth.

Continue to heat over MED heat, whisking very often, until thickened to a very thick consistency. It should almost be the consistency of a semi thinned out condensed soup.
Remove from the heat and stir in spices and 1 1/2 cups of the cheeses, stirring to melt and combine. Stir in another 1 1/2 cups of cheese, and stir until completely melted and smooth.

In a large mixing bowl, combine drained pasta with cheese sauce, stirring to combine fully. Pour half of the pasta mixture into the prepared baking dish, skillet, or individual baking dishes. Top with 1 1/2 cups of grated cheeses, then top that with the remaining pasta mixture.

Sprinkle the top with the last 1 1/2 cups of cheese and any other toppings. Bake for 15 minutes, until cheesy is bubbly and lightly golden brown.

Mariah's Berry Streusel Muffins

3 large eggs
1 1/2 cup milk
1 teaspoon pure vanilla extract
3 cups all-purpose flour
1 cup granulated white sugar
2 1/2 teaspoons baking powder
pinch of salt
1/8 teaspoon ground cinnamon (optional)
1/2 cup cold unsalted butter, cut into small chunks
2 cups fresh berries of your choice*
2 tablespoons unsalted butter
* You can dust them lightly with flour; this helps prevent the berries from "bleeding" into the muffins.

Preheat the oven to 375°F. Lightly grease a standard 12-cup muffin tin; or line the tin with papers, and grease the papers.

For Muffins
In a medium sized bowl, whisk the eggs with the milk and vanilla extract.

In a large mixing bowl, whisk the flour with the sugar, baking powder, salt, and ground cinnamon. Cut the butter into the flour mixture with a pastry blender or your fingertips. (The mixture should look like coarse crumbs.)

Remove one cup of the mixture and set aside in a separate bowl to make the streusel topping.

Add the milk and egg mixture to the flour mixture. Stir just until combined.

Fill each muffin cup about 3/4 full with the batter, using two spoons or an ice cream scoop.

Cover the batter with the berries and then cover the berries with streusel topping.

Streusel Topping
Melt the remaining 2 tablespoons butter and stir into the reserved one cup of flour mixture until it is crumbly and looks like coarse meal. Sprinkle about 1 tablespoon of the streusel on top of each muffin.

Bake the muffins for about 20-25 minutes, until they're light golden brown on top, and a toothpick inserted into the middle of one of the center muffins comes out clean.

Remove the muffins from the oven, loosen their edges from the pan, and after about 5 minutes transfer them to a rack to cool.

Check out the next book in the series:
Half Hitch

Rebecca Connolly writes romances, both period and contemporary, because she absolutely loves a good love story. She has been creating stories since childhood, and there are home videos to prove it! She started writing them down in elementary school and has never looked back. She currently lives in Indiana, spends every spare moment away from her day job absorbed in her writing, and is a hot cocoa addict.

www.ingramcontent.com/pod-product-compliance
Lightning Source LLC
LaVergne TN
LVHW021809060526
838201LV00058B/3305